STAR TREK®
Aliens & Artifacts

STAR TREK®
Aliens & Artifacts

MICHAEL WESTMORE

ALAN SIMS

BRADLEY M. LOOK

WILLIAM J. BIRNES

POCKET BOOKS

New York   London   Toronto   Sydney   Singapore

POCKET BOOKS, a division of Simon & Schuster, Inc.
1230 Avenue of the Americas, New York, NY 10020

Copyright © 2000 by Paramount Pictures. All Rights Reserved.

 STAR TREK is a Registered Trademark of Paramount Pictures.

This book is published by Pocket Books, a division of Simon & Schuster, Inc.,
under exclusive license from Paramount Pictures.

All rights reserved, including the right to reproduce this book or portions thereof in any
form whatsoever. For information address Pocket Books, 1230 Avenue of the Americas,
New York, NY, 10020

ISBN: 0-671-04299-8

First Pocket Books trade paperback printing October 2000

10 9 8 7 6 5 4 3 2 1

POCKET and colophon are registered trademarks of Simon & Schuster, Inc.

Printed in the U.S.A.

TO RICK BERMAN

What most people don't realize is how one person's steady hand has shaped what we understand as *Star Trek*. All of us who have been privileged to work with him usually stand as silent witnesses to this man's genius. But we each know that it is his steadfast insistence on nothing less than the very best from *everyone* connected with the shows and movies that has shaped *Star Trek* into the unprecedented phenomenon that it is today.

It may be our work, you see, but it is his vision that *is Star Trek*.

Contents

Introduction

Before filming started on the pilot episode of *Star Trek: The Next Generation*, I received a cast, staff, and crew list from the production office. Among the scores of names there were only three that I recognized; LeVar Burton, Wil Wheaton, and Michael Westmore. LeVar because of *Roots*, Wil for *Stand by Me*, and Michael Westmore for... well, what? The Westmore name I knew well enough from countless films, going all the way back to my earliest moviegoing. I had seen the names Monty, Perc, and Frank Westmore and I had assumed they were a family. I didn't know they were a dynasty. On that production list the name Michael Westmore was down as Head of Makeup Department. That was all I needed to know. I would be working with a man whose family name was linked with the whole history of film-making in Hollywood. I didn't know that I would also be working with an artist, an inventor, a visionary, a fantasist. I later discovered he was also an extraordinarily nice man, a generous man, a raconteur, and a chocolate addict.

My makeup for *TNG* could not have been more simple and straightforward, therefore there was no need for Michael to focus his special talents on me. I passed through the hands of several different makeup artists in my first season—not, I hope, because I was difficult. Occasionally Michael would do my makeup or "touch me up" and I always felt a certain sense of privilege at those times, having his hands on my face. Eventually, however, as the writers became bolder with the character of Picard my appearance had to change; more youthful—with a hairpiece for "Violations"; more aged for the series finale "All Good Things..."; extremely aged for "Inner Light"; Romulan for "Unification"; a character for the holodeck fifteenth-century soldier Williams. (It was a bit of a cheat my playing this role but Rick Berman agreed with me that it would be fun to hide the good captain behind this small, supporting Shakespearean role. Unfortunately, despite Michael's skills too many people spotted it was me.) Michael took charge of those special makeups.

I always enjoyed these transformations—watching in the mirror as the different stages of the process were reached and the familiar features of Patrick Stewart disappeared. What I found interesting was that with the altered appearance there came an altered feeling about who I was, how I moved, how I talked. Michael's makeup design satisfied that deep and ancient impulse in an actor to "dress up" and become somebody else.

Of course, I never got to wear one of the more extreme and "alien" of Michael's designs. I wish I'd had the chance. Maybe I will in some future "guest" appearance. I did, however, get to work often with many of these aliens and it was always fascinating, particularly as I usually only met these actors once they were in costume and makeup. I believed in them. They were very convincing. I always had to remind myself, however, that I was Jean-Luc Picard and Jean-Luc would never stare inquisitively at an alien or intrude on his or her body space. Sometimes the toughest thing was behaving quite naturally when confronted with a very unhuman-like or an occasionally quite terrifying creature. Michael's designs were never mere fantasy. There was

always a feeling of a skeleton and cell structure just below the surface. These makeups breathed, and blood—or something—ran in their veins. I even sensed there was a particular odor to some of our aliens. The Bynars I felt would be sweet-smelling whereas the Cardassians, I am sure, were too foul to want to get close to. (Any Cardassian reading this, please don't take it personally.) I was very fond of the Bynars—maybe it was their pretty dancers' bodies—and wished that we had met them more than once.

As I have mentioned, only rarely did I have to spend an extended time in the makeup chair. I would boast that I could go from my street clothes to "set ready" in around twelve minutes, if pushed. Nevertheless, and I think to the irritation of some of my more extensively made-up colleagues, I hold the record for the earliest call and the longest makeup on *TNG*. That was for the most aged appearance of my character in "Inner Light." My makeup call was 1:00 A.M. and took a full six hours. I slept some of the time, as Michael would work away in a manner that was soothing and sleep inducing. But

if I needed to be entertained or distracted Michael could regale me not only with fascinating stories about his father and uncles and the founder of the dynasty—the tyrannical, brilliant, and tragic George—but also Hollywood gossip, about which makeup artists know more than anyone else. Michael also loves the good life and his dish-by-dish account of his previous evening's dinner was always amusing and mouth-watering.

It is not possible to think of *Star Trek* without thinking of Mike Westmore, his dedication to the spirit of *Trek*, and his very healthy irony about it all. His bottomless inventiveness and humor. His stamina. Study the hours this man put in on the set, in the makeup trailer, in his studio or his office and you will be exhausted at the very thought of it. But above all, for those of us who stumbled into the make-up trailer five days a week, while most of the rest of the West Coast was just opening its curtains on a new day, seeing Michael already cheerfully and busily working away was a comfort and inspiration.

—Patrick Stewart

CHAPTER ONE

The Pilots

"THE CAGE" AND "WHERE NO MAN HAS GONE BEFORE"

Fred B. Phillips watched carefully from the shadows behind a camera on Desilu's Sound Stage 16 at the studio in Culver City as the first take of the day, Scene 15 in the transporter room of the Enterprise, was about to begin. Already in position on the transporter pads, Captain Pike, Mr. Spock, Tyler, and Boyce were waiting to beam down to the surface of Talos IV in response to a distress call from a science vessel that had crashed years earlier. Fred Phillips, the head of makeup for what he and the show's creator, Gene Roddenberry, hoped would become a regular series, looked at the characters for any beads of sweat under the hot lights. Phillips was especially concerned about the pointed ears on the actor Leonard Nimoy, who was playing Spock, the alien on the bridge crew whose makeup was particularly critical to the look of the new show. Even a hint that the appliances on his ears were slipping, a seam between the rubber and the glue, would be enough to ruin the entire shot. But the scene went on, Pike and his team rematerialized on the surface of Talos IV, and the first scenes of Star Trek were laid down on film.

What was unfolding before the eyes of the cast and crew on the day after Thanksgiving, November 27, 1964, was something brand-new, a type of science fiction that owed more to the television adult Westerns of the late 1950s and C. S. Forrester's Horatio Hornblower novels than to the action-adventure science fiction shows of early television. The genre had been popular throughout the 1950s, evolving into *The Outer Limits* in the early 1960s, which set a standard for the

His primary weakness is an almost catlike curiosity over anything the slightest "alien."

The understated makeup for Spock made it easier for the audience to accept this alien character.

Courtesy of the Gregory Jein Collection

but definitely an extraterrestrial, was a Vulcan Starfleet officer named Spock, whose makeup would go through several transformations before the show finally found its way onto the airwaves.

In creating Spock, Roddenberry wanted to reinforce the notion that there is always an alien presence on the show. But at the heart of the matter, Roddenberry wanted a different perspective, that of an outsider looking in, a "stranger in a strange land." Makeup was vital to the creation of Spock's character because it was important that Spock not only act different, but look different, without being bizarre or monstrous. Also, Spock had to represent a clean break from 1950s science fiction features; no skintight space suits or oversized helmets. Spock was a real character and not a piece of alien comic relief.

Accordingly, the artistry of makeup and hair would be an essential component of Spock, as well of the other *Star Trek* aliens. But it was the early 1960s, and what Roddenberry was asking for was difficult to accomplish given the shooting schedule of an episodic television series and the types of makeup and appliances available at that time. Even a short time spent watching reruns of *The Outer Limits* episodes from the early 1960s will reveal the kinds of makeup devices typically used to create an otherworldly look for alien characters. Roddenberry wanted Spock to be able to amalgamate into the rest of the bridge crew yet stand out just enough to be recognized as an alien. And Spock's character had to have the same range of movement as the human characters. This was a challenge.

look of otherworldly creatures, bizarre aliens, and odd-looking props.

Critical to Roddenberry's vision of the future was the look of his characters, the costuming and the equipment they carried, and the makeup design of the aliens. From the very start, Roddenberry wanted one of the regular characters on the *Enterprise* bridge crew to be an alien, part his concept for a multi-ethnic, multi-species future of humanity. The alien on the bridge, humanlike in many respects

In Roddenberry's first description of Spock in the show's bible, he wrote:

> *The First Lieutenant. The Captain's right-hand man, the working-level commander of all the ship's functions—ranging from manning the bridge to supervising the lowliest scrub detail. His name is Mr. Spock. And the first view of him can be almost frightening—a face so heavy-lidded and satanic you might almost expect him to have a forked tail. Probably half Martian, he has a slightly reddish complexion and semi-pointed ears. But strangely— Mr. Spock's quiet temperament is in dramatic contrast to his satanic look. Of all the crew aboard, he is the nearest to Captain April's equal, physically and emotionally, and as a commander of men. His primary weakness is an almost catlike curiosity over anything the slightest "alien."*

Spock was originally conceived as a red-skinned alien, according to Samuel A. Peeples, the author of *Star Trek*'s second pilot, "Where No Man Has Gone Before." In an interview in *The Star Trek Interview Book* Peeples recalls that Spock had fiery ears and a plate in the middle of his stomach. He didn't eat or drink, but he fed upon any form of energy that struck this stomach plate. Peeples told Roddenberry that in his opinion this effectively destroyed Spock as an interesting character, because he was no longer a recognizable human being. It was Peeples's idea, he told the interviewer, that Spock should be half human and have problems resulting from both sides of his character and personality.

Roddenberry took Peeples's advice and brought Spock back to a more human look. He was also being realistic, because the makeup budget didn't allow for the re-creation of exotic designs that would reinvent the makeup industry. They had to use what they had, rely on the resources of the studio as well as out-source to companies that could work on very tight budgets. The budget restrictions also meant that, as much as possible, conventional makeup would have to define the look of aliens. The fundamental differences between aliens and humans would be best represented by different habits and conventions that would be translated into story. As Roddenberry wrote in the show's bible:

> *Alien Life. Normal production casting of much of this alien is made practical by the SIMILAR WORLDS CONCEPT. To give continual variety, use will, of course, have to be made of wigs, skin coloration, changes in noses, hands, ears, and even the occasional addition of tails and such.*
>
> *As exciting as physical differences, and often even more so, will be the universe's incredible differences in social organizations, customs, habit, nourishment, religion, sex, politics, morals, intellect, locomotion, family life, emotions, etc.*

Also for Roddenberry, the look of aliens and strange new worlds on *Star Trek* was defined by the still infant technology of broadcasting a show in color. A majority of household television sets were still black-and-white. NBC was one of the first networks to have a color television series,

...Roddenberry had to convince his network that Star Trek had to be in color. NBC was reluctant to make a commitment to color in 1964 because of the expense and the lack of an audience for the new show.

gambling that the popularity of *Bonanza* would sell the concept of color television to America's growing television audience. But by 1964 there was still a lot of uncertainty as to how well television would pick up subtle color skin tones.

Makeup artist Frank Westmore was one of the early explorers in the field of makeup for color television. He was hired by Paramount, where *Bonanza* was filmed, to run a series of color makeup tests to see how full-color makeup transmitted. His experiment also had to determine the colors most compatible with black-and-white so that broadcasting in color didn't make the images on a black-and-white set look so indistinct that it turned away viewers. For example, if an artist applied a fantasy makeup using bright reds, greens, or blues, they could look indistinguishable on a black-and-white set. So the television production studios needed a color-compatibility chart. Frank Westmore devised a chart, which quickly became a benchmark for color to black-and-white compatibility.

First, Gene Roddenberry had to convince his network that *Star Trek* had to be in color. NBC was reluctant to make a commitment to color in 1964 because of the expense and the lack of an audience for the new show. Roddenberry explained to the network that one of the most important premises of the show's

artistic and makeup design was color. He explained that it would make no sense for the *Enterprise* to visit strange new worlds only to find that the atmosphere looked the same shades of gray. By the simple use of color filters and lighting gels, the blue sky of Earth would become the red sky of Mars without expensive set design. Color would solve a multitude of production issues.

Color was not only a more effective way to deliver the show's premise, Roddenberry argued, it added a dimension of believability to the series that could not be conveyed in black-and-white. Without color, how could he show the distinction between aliens and humans without expensive and bizarre makeup appliances? If Mr. Spock was red-toned, how would that show up in gray? And how could Vina, the green-skinned yet otherwise perfectly human Orion slave girl, appear to be an exotic alien when she was only a deeper shade of gray in black-and-white? When NBC agreed to finance a color production, Roddenberry moved on to the next issues, the casting and final makeup of Mr. Spock.

After selecting Leonard Nimoy to play Spock, Roddenberry had to work the look of the alien into something believable within the restrictions of his budget. He hired Lee Greenway, the creator of the monster in Howard Hawks's 1951 film *The Thing*, as the production company's makeup artist, whose first assignment was the design of the alien Mr. Spock. Leonard Nimoy and Greenway had worked together before, in a small feature called *Kid Monk Baroni* years earlier. Greenway first tried to manipulate some papier-mâché, and then literally poured liquid latex over Nimoy's ears. With no budget and no time to prepare, the prefabricated appliances that Greenway would have liked to create just weren't available. He had to build this character on the spot from scratch.

Pressing on, Greenway next covered up the outer half of Nimoy's eyebrows with mortician's wax and began the painstaking process of gluing a new eyebrow, this time slanted up toward the pointed ears. Then came the deep-reddish-tint skin dye, and Spock was ready for his first screen makeup test. The test was shot on the set of *The Lucy Show*, which was being taped later that evening. As the cameras rolled film, Nimoy turned his head to the left and right, capturing as many angles of the alien makeup as possible for this first test, which would tell the producers if they'd achieved the alien look they were after.

But this first stab at alien makeup didn't work. On the color monitors the makeup looked passable, but for the majority of homes that still had black-and-white televisions, Leonard Nimoy looked like he was wearing pasty Halloween makeup. Roddenberry decided that the color base had to be changed for the next screen test. He also wanted other changes to make the character look less like he was a human being wearing funny appliances and more like a humanoid whose features were just different enough to make it clear that he was not of this Earth. Oscar Katz, the president of Desilu, wrote a memo to Roddenberry that read:

> EAR: Tone down the pointed ear. It should be cupped more so as to create a more natural look.
>
> HAIR: Should have a bowl shaped haircut with a frayed or jagged look.
>
> EYEBROWS: Should be shaped so as to lead up toward the ears.

Roddenberry next memoed his production team that they needed to find a permanent makeup man with experience in network television series and an ability to create designs for alien characters in a science fiction series. "Is it possible," Roddenberry wrote, "to get a blend of these two qualities?"

Robert Justman, recently hired by Roddenberry as the assistant director and associate producer for "The Cage," knew you needed someone who understood the intricacies of television production but appreciated the complexities of special makeup. Justman also understood that *Star Trek* needed someone with experience in other science fiction television shows who was capable of setting up his own shop within the production unit, because Desilu Studios had no makeup department. All makeup, except for Lucille Ball's makeup, was done on portable tables right on the set. The new makeup director had to establish what amounted to his own department.

Bob Justman chose Fred Phillips to take over makeup, in part because the two of them had worked together on *The Outer Limits*, and Justman knew that Fred Phillips understood the genre of science fiction and the importance of not having his extraterrestrials look like the aliens of 1950s B movies. Phillips had also developed a series of prosthetics and appliances that could be mixed and matched and that helped manage a makeup and effects budget that could have gotten out of control.

Time was very tight as the *Star Trek* team approached the first day of shooting for the pilot. Spock's makeup had to be fixed, and Phillips had another major test to perform. It was on the character of Vina transformed by the Talosians into the green-skinned Orion slave girl. This was an especially important test, almost as important as Spock, because the appearance of the slave girl had to sell the tension of the scene by shaking the reserve of Captain Pike, who must refuse to succumb to the intense sexuality of the mate selected for him by his keepers, the Talosians. As the script described Vina:

Wild! Green skin, glistening as if oiled. Her fingertips are long gleaming razor-edge scimitars, her hair not unattractive but suggesting a wild animal mane. She is moving out to the open rectangle in front of the table, eyes wild. We feel she's larger than before, immensely strong. The female slaves have hurried off, frightened. But one is slower and Vina suddenly pivots with a CAT SOUND, bars a frightened female slave's escape.

This was a critical test of how the green would look in color as well as black-and-white. However, because actress Susan Oliver had not yet been selected to play the role, the only woman on the set was the actress playing Captain Pike's first officer, Number One, Majel Barrett. She agreed to be the stand-in for the test.

In those days of early color television, the processing of the film could make colors read very differently from the way they were shot. As a result, the early television makeup artists went through much the same processes as their feature-film counterparts did in the early days of Technicolor. But for Gene Roddenberry and Fred Phillips, this was a first. No one

had ever tried to make an actress green on television before, and not even Fred Phillips was sure how it would turn out.

Phillips applied several different shades of green greasepaint to Majel's face and arms before she was set up on Stage 15, where she was to be photographed in front of a neutral gray backdrop. Then, in test after test, they shot footage of Majel at different exposures and with different changes to the lighting on the set. They experimented with different angles to see how the green would register under a variety of conditions, especially because of the dance sequence. Then they wrapped for the day and waited. And the next morning, the dailies arrived from the lab.

As a shocked production team watched the footage in the Desilu screening room, a beige flesh-toned Majel Barrett showed off her invisible pigment to the camera. There was no green at all. What had gone wrong? Maybe it was the Eastman negative film, Justman thought, that couldn't replicate the color green. But Phillips knew it had to be something else, something in the makeup. But he couldn't figure out what it could be. Why wouldn't standard green greasepaint show up on this film the way it had shown up in scores of Westerns for the past ten years?

Gene Roddenberry said the pigment was probably too light and asked Fred to use a deeper value of green for the next day's test. But, although Fred saturated the greasepaint with deeper and deeper shades of green on the next day's test, the dailies still came back beige the following morning. And the same thing happened on the third day of testing, even though Fred tried as many combinations of green pigment as he could think of. As green as Majel was painted, she looked normal in the next morning's dailies. It simply made no sense.

In frustration, Roddenberry finally

"You mean she was supposed to be green? ... We were up half the night correcting for the green."

called the color lab to see what kinds of filters he could use or different arrangements of lighting and gels to get the green skin color he wanted.

"You mean she was supposed to be green?" one of the lab technicians asked. "We thought the cinematographer had the camera settings all wrong so we retimed the print so the actress would look regular. We were up half the night correcting for the green."

With the problem of the Orion slave girl's skin tone settled, Fred Phillips turned to Spock's skin tone. The red tint had been abandoned, because on black-and-white screens Nimoy's face was jet black against his black hair. Instead, Phillips ordered "Chinese" makeup from Max Factor, a yellowish green that made Spock look alien on a color monitor and slightly off-gray in black-and-white. His eyebrows, now fashioned out of hand-laid yak hair, were working out, and the bowl-shaped haircut and pointed sideburns made him look different from the rest of the crew. But the ears were still a problem.

Fred Phillips didn't think that Projects Unlimited, the company commissioned by Desilu for all the props and alien costumes, was capable of fabricating a finely crafted set of ear appliances. So, rather than spend the two or three days before the first shooting day fighting with the studio, he threw out the latest set of ears from Projects Unlimited and called Charlie Schram at MGM, asking whether the master appliance designer could figure out how to make a pair of foam latex Peter Pan ears in less than two days. Schram said he needed Leonard's ears to

work on, so Fred took him over to MGM, where Schram made a cast of Nimoy's ears and fitted them with perfectly formed tips.

By the first day of shooting, Phillips was fitting the new appliances to Leonard Nimoy's ears and gluing them into place with Max Factor spirit gum to blend the edge of the appliance on to the skin. Leonard's ear points still stuck out too far, so before he got him onto the set, Phillips used double-sided toupee tape on the backside edges of Leonard's ears to affix them to the side of his head. That way the pointed ears looked normal—normal for an alien.

Fred Phillips does one of his innumerable touch-ups on Susan Oliver as the Orion slave girl.

Courtesy of the Gregory Jein Collection

Part of Wah's genius was the development of what would become known as the "bladder effect," which was essentially a makeup prop that turned the thought communication of the Talosians into a visual effect.

Gene Roddenberry (center) watches as Bob Justman (right) inflates the bladder in the Keeper's head.

Courtesy of the Gregory Jein Collection

Phillips watched as Pike, Spock, and the rest of the team completed the scene in the transporter room. His creation, Spock, had finally come together. His skin tone and ears made it possible for Spock to blend with the rest of the bridge crew as if he had always been there. In a sense, it allowed the audience to accept an extraterrestrial as a hero instead of a monster. But even as the morning's shooting ended, Phillips's next project would be already heading over to Desilu for the makeup test. It was the Talosians, Meg Wyllie, Georgia Schmidt, and Selena Sande, a novel experiment in casting and makeup.

Originally, the Talosians had been described in the treatment as crablike creatures. But as the script evolved from the treatment it became obvious that crab creatures, even if they didn't look like throwbacks to 1950s B horror movies, lacked the credibility and mobility to deliver the subtle message of the story and would be too expensive given the amount of stage time and interaction with the other characters that they required. The Talosians had to be humanoid without being human; more alien than Mr. Spock, but not too alien to look incongruous as a rescuer and then keeper of Vina. Also, the aliens had to have a perceived weakness that would challenge and even frustrate Christopher Pike until he found the key to their undoing.

During preproduction, Roddenberry and his director, Robert Butler, came up with the idea of casting women as unisex aliens. Women brought a delicacy and fragility that went beyond makeup and wardrobe. Now the trick was to create a makeup that would make the Talosians seem ominous even though they were smaller and much less physically formidable than Captain Pike. Accordingly, Roddenberry decided to give them enormous bald heads with minute ears. This allowed the characters to remain diminutive and almost non-threatening because of their size, but still inspire an otherworldly fear because they looked alien.

The Talosians were the creation of Projects Unlimited chief designer and partner Wah Ming Chang, one of the most legendary makeup and prop designers in Hollywood. Wah Chang, who would later design some of the most famous aliens on the *Star Trek* series, had already been designing alien creatures and monsters for *The Outer Limits* when he was hired to fabricate the huge foam latex heads for the Talosians. Part of Wah's genius was the development of what would become known as the "bladder effect," which was essentially a makeup prop that turned the thought communication of the Talosians into a visual effect.

To create a piece of stage business as a visual counterpart to the Talosian dialogue, Roddenberry needed an effect to show

that the Talosians were actually doing something when they projected their thoughts into the minds of their subjects. Wah Chang accomplished this by creating a rubber bladder device that looked like a large vein just beneath the skin on the Talosian's forehead. The bladder was controlled by means of a flexible tube that ran down the back of the appliance neck and underneath the loosely flowing costume to a long tube that was connected to a rubber squeeze bulb held by Bob Justman below the camera. Keeping time with the dialogue, Justman squeezed the bulb, which expanded the vein in the Talosian's forehead and gave the illusion of a pulsating vein as the Talosian's thoughts were projected into the brains of its captives.

The final lead role was filled when Susan Oliver was cast to play Vina. Phillips quickly discovered that making a person's face green was a lot easier than making up a whole body. Greasepaint creases and cracks as it folds upon itself. After the first few setups, Susan began to streak, and then she turned blotchy. Phillips had to have her retouched before every new setup so the makeup would stay even.

Later on in the episode Susan Oliver went through another, equally famous, makeup change. The Talosians revealed to Christopher Pike the true appearance of Vina, a badly wrinkled, maimed, scarred, and deformed accident victim whose injuries were beyond the Talosian medical expertise to repair. The beautiful young woman who had wooed Pike was only an illusion. How to not only create the look of a twisted and mangled victim but to achieve the transformation right on camera? That was the challenge that faced Fred Phillips and the production team.

The first step was to shoot a few feet of film of beautiful Susan as a "lock-down" shoot, a camera in a fixed position so there'd be no indication that the actor had moved during the transformation. Susan herself was "locked" into position by a head brace that prevented any movement from shot to shot. In other words, each time she returned with new makeup she'd be photographed in exactly the same position as the previous shot. After the initial footage of the alluring Vina, Susan left the set—a "hot set" on which nothing was allowed to be touched—for a makeup change. Fred stippled liquid latex onto Susan's eyelids, which were stretched down to prevent the latex from sticking to itself during the application. Then a coating of powder was applied to her eyelids to prevent them from sticking when they were released. All of this created a wrinkled, drooping effect, making her look tired, sick, and in pain. When Fred Phillips

added shading to her eyes and shadows to her face, she looked drawn and old— the antithesis of the vital young woman Captain Pike thought she was.

With the first stage of her new makeup applied, Susan was returned to the set, where she was again put into the head brace. Now a few more feet of film were shot and she went back to the makeup chair. This time Fred molded a broken nose for the actress out of latex, more shadows were applied, the faintest outlines of a scar were applied across her forehead, and a device was inserted into the left side of her mouth to draw it down. Then it was back to the set for a few more feet of film before she was returned for the next phase of the makeup.

Now, Vina's scars were deepened and, with the insertion of a prosthetic foam hump device beneath her costume, her body looked broken. Back to the set and

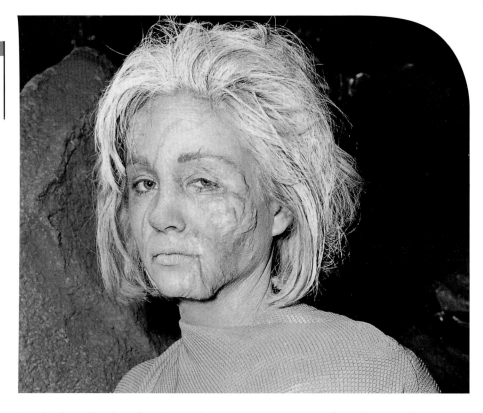

then back to the chair for a larger hump to complete the physical disfiguration, the application of latex growths on her face to make her truly grotesque without becoming bizarre, and more discoloration to complete the effect. By the time she was returned to the lock-in position on the set for the final piece of photography, she had become something pitiable and monstrous at the same time. When the transformation footage was edited, the result was about fifteen seconds of one dissolve after another in one of the most memorable sequences in all of *Star Trek*.

But for all that work, and all that money, NBC rejected the final version of "The Cage." "Too cerebral," they called it, and they still didn't buy the character of Spock. They felt his pointed ears would offend religious members of the television audience. Moreover, they were unhappy with a female Number One who, they said, didn't relate to the mostly male test audience. Men found her too threatening, the network said; they actually hated the character.

However, the network was so impressed with the concept of *Star Trek* that they gave Roddenberry the green light for another pilot, provided that he stayed with a substantially reduced budget and turned in three new scripts prior to shooting the second pilot. There would be no new sets, because of the expense involved in creating the first *Enterprise* and Talos IV, and the network capped Roddenberry's production budget at $300,000.

Roddenberry submitted "Where No Man Has Gone Before," by Samuel A. Peeples, the script that would become the second pilot; "The Omega Glory," which Roddenberry wrote himself; and "Mudd's Women," the teleplay by Stephen Kandel from a story by Roddenberry. While innovative, "Mudd's Women" was more of a cerebral comedy and not science fiction enough for the network. "Omega Glory" carried too much back-story for a pilot episode. Of the three scripts, "Where No Man Has Gone Before" was a straight-line science fiction adventure, which was exactly what the network was looking for.

Roddenberry's first battle with the network was over the character of Spock. Fighting hard, he got the network to agree with him that Mr. Spock was vital: he embodied the very essence of the new science fiction that *Star Trek* represented, an alien presence amid a crew of humans in a century where extraterrestrial creatures were part of a greater galactic society. As part of the bargain, Roddenberry surrendered Number One and transferred her cold, logical demeanor to Spock. Roddenberry also agreed to keep Spock in the background, not give him too many lines, and transform him into more of a visual presence than a critical member of the crew. As a result, the Mr. Spock of the second pilot emerges as just the first officer. The second pilot also featured the arrival of William Shatner as Captain James T. Kirk, the new captain of the *Enterprise*.

Fred Phillips was not available to do the second pilot, so Robert Dawn was hired. He set to work on a new set of ears for Spock and a more conventional bowl haircut. The result was a more human and moderate-looking Spock. Dawn also had to do his job on a sharply reduced budget. Roddenberry and Dawn were working hard against the clock because the network wanted a fast production of the pilot even on the reduced budget. As a result, and building on what he had learned on "The Cage," Roddenberry came up with a new set of guidelines for how he wanted the makeup team to work. In his "Department and Crew Comments" memo, he wrote:

8. MAKEUP

a. **Construction of makeup room**

Considerable time was lost here. We need white walls and ceilings, hot and cold running water, adequate lights, hair dryer, shampoo basin and any other equipment usual for complicated makeup and hairstyling jobs. If at all possible, the makeup man should supervise the construction and furnishing of the makeup room. Very important, he would be allowed to supervise the placement of all lights. The actor must be made up for a lit stage rather than for a poorly lit makeup room. The difference was quite apparent when making up characters such as the Talosians. Makeup too often had to be corrected on the stage due to the difference in lighting.

b. **Unusual hand makeup jobs**

Avoid involved hand makeup jobs such as six fingers, glass hands, et cetera. It takes two to three times longer than regular makeup jobs.

c. **Use of actresses**

Whenever doing a time-consuming episode, we should limit the use of females. Since other aspects of the show can be very time-consuming, we cannot often afford the forty-five minutes per actress lost each day in hairstyling time. Also, whenever possible, avoid hiring actresses with very long hair, as a great deal of time consumed in creating workable hairstyles. It also eats up time each time the hair has to be restyled to match a previous day's scene.

d. **Unusual face makeup**

On any makeup job involving complex face makeup such as enlarged faces, distorted features, lack of eyes, etc., have a mold make of the actor's face. Using the mold, the makeup man can, without the use of the actor, experiment with different forms of makeup appliances. The use of the mold serves two purposes. One, it eliminates the need of calling the actor in for makeup tests, and secondly, it allows the makeup man time before actual production to perfect his makeup.

e.   Use of a makeup laboratory

Whenever planning to manufacture items such as the Talosian heads, use of a makeup laboratory should be explored. While the initial cost may be twice that of a prop shop, the money and time saved in the makeup room and on the stage will more than compensate for the increased cost. By having the Talosian heads manufactured by a makeup laboratory, they would be designed and constructed using a human model having the same dimensions as that of the actor. This permits the technician to make the head, using an animate model, and allowing him to compensate for the quick movements normally made by a human head. When in actual use, instead of taking two and a half hours, the head could be affixed and made up on the working actor in less than twenty-five minutes. Over a period of days, the head will more than pay for itself.

Roddenberry's guidelines for "Where No Man Has Gone Before" became working procedures for the ensuing series and for the series that followed. Even on today's *Star Trek: Voyager*, while there have been almost quantum leaps in the types of materials used for makeup and appliances, molds of performers' heads are still the basis for applying makeup quickly and experimenting with different variations of makeup.

"Where No Man Has Gone Before" featured glowing eyes of two crew members struck with a mysterious beam. Lt. Gary Mitchell and Dr. Elizabeth Dehner are transforming into alien beings, ultimately endowed with supernatural powers, shown by the strange glowing light that emanates from their eyes. For middle-1960s technology, before the days of custom-designed and soft contact lenses, glowing eyes were quite an achievement. Bob Justman tracked down an optician, John Roberts, who fabricated the silver-colored contact lenses. Justman explained the effect he was trying to create, and the optician asked for the weekend to see what he could come up with.

Although there was an initial misunderstanding about whether the actors were to be able to see through the lenses, by

the time actors Gary Lockwood and Sally Kellerman were fitted with the lenses, they were ready to shoot the episode. Sally Kellerman's lenses fit fine. However, Gary Lockwood's lenses were not fitted properly, and he found that in order to see, he had to raise his head and look down through the openings in the lenses. Although this was awkward at first, this gave his performance an attitude of superiority, as if he were looking down at the rest of mortal humanity, and provided the pilot with an aspect of reality that couldn't have been planned.

In addition to the silver lenses, Robert Dawn and hairstylist Hazel Keats gradually colored Gary Lockwood's hair progressively more at the temples as he mutated into more of a demonic creature bent on destroying Kirk and reducing his shipmates to slaves. Stage blood, glycerin-based stage sweat, and other effects were also used during the climactic fight scene between Kirk and Mitchell before Dehner came to Kirk's rescue by sacrificing herself.

"Where No Man Has Gone Before" did not have a large prop budget. However, the communicators, tricorder, and phasers created by artist Wah Ming Chang have become cultural icons. For the second pilot, Chang created the design for the

phaser rifle, an obvious modification of the hand phaser.

What is most astounding about the first two *Star Trek* pilots is that despite what modern audiences would call a primitive look, both the makeup and the props were among the most advanced for any series on television. Within the strict constraints of budget, the *Star Trek* production team utilized almost everything it had developed for "The Cage,"

The use of everday items—manual-typewriter keys for control studs on the phaser and wire mesh for the communicator—is exactly what was done for all the ensuing *Star Trek* television series. Wah Chang's concept of re-utilizing the everyday designs and materials for different props was still the practice for the property masters on *Star Trek: The Next Generation*, *Star Trek: Deep Space Nine*, and *Star Trek: Voyager*.

A hand phaser from the pilot.
Courtesy of the
Gregory Jein Collection

Wah Ming Chang prided himself on his ability to recognize special qualities of materials, even the most mundane types of materials, to incorporate them into "alien" devices.

and was innovative in the one effect that set both Mitchell and Dehner apart from the rest of the crew. Also, Wah Chang's ability to turn common hardware-store and household items into components of futuristic weapons and communicators helped the producers stay within budget.

Wah Ming Chang prided himself on his ability to recognize special qualities of materials, even the most mundane types of materials, to incorporate them into "alien" devices. Partly, Chang has explained, it was the function of the object that defined the look, and that was how the prop was created. A hand phaser had to look like a gun first. The design for the communicator came from the handheld toy walkie-talkies that were common in the 1950s. Wah's creation of the flip wire mesh, however, turned the device into a design that echoes today's cell phones.

"Where No Man Has Gone Before" was a streamlined and elegant production far ahead of what other television series were even attempting to accomplish in 1965. Roddenberry's concept of an alien crew member as the first officer, women as equal members of the crew, and the story of ultimate power ultimately corrupting the human spirit made the second pilot a successful beginning for the longest-running television franchise in history. Of course, no one would know the outcome of the network's decision until more than seven months after shooting. In February 1966, *Star Trek* was finally green-lighted for the fall season.

Fred Phillips

Fred Phillips was not only the godfather of Mr. Spock but the artist who designed the looks of the first Klingons, Andorians, Romulans, and Tellarites. Fred came to Hollywood in 1911 with his family after his father, Festus Phillips, was persuaded by D. W. Griffith to become a silent-film actor. Soon, however, Festus Phillips found himself in demand by other actors who liked the way he had applied his own makeup. Festus became a makeup artist and taught the skill to his sons William and Fred. Fred developed his skill working in such silent-film classics as Ben Hur *and* King of Kings *and was also known for his work on* One Flew Over the Cuckoo's Nest. *On television, Phillips helped develop the look of the bizarre characters on* The Outer Limits *where he met and collaborated with Wah Ming Chang. Fred Phillips died in 1993.*

Robert Dawn

Robert Dawn, who died in 1983, was the son of Jack Dawn, the Director of Makeup at MGM. After World War II, Robert returned to Hollywood to apprentice under his father at MGM, where he remained until 1954. In addition to conventional makeup techniques, Robert became skilled in lab work, which was in great demand during the 1950s and '60s. Dawn's work was seen in The Creature from the Black Lagoon *and* This Island Earth *where he worked with Bud Westmore. On This Island Earth, Dawn assisted in the creation of the huge brain-exposed head for the extraterrestrial mutant who threatens the human survivors as they make their way back toward Earth in the alien spaceship.*
In television, Dawn worked on the early horror series Thriller, *and* Wagon Train *before he did the second pilot for* Star Trek.

Wah Ming Chang

By the time he was only eight years old, Wah Chang was described as an artistic prodigy by the New York Times *for the critical praise his art exhibits had gathered. A native of Hawaii, Wah found early work in pictures at Walt Disney Studios in the effects and model departments, where he worked on* Fantasia, Pinocchio, *and* Bambi. *In 1960, Wah Chang shared the Academy Award for his design and manufacture of George Pal's vision of the H. G. Wells time machine. By 1963 he was working on* The Outer Limits. *However, it was his prop designs—communicator, phaser, and tricorder—as well as some of his aliens in the original series episodes of* Star Trek, *that have become his most famous work.*

CHAPTER TWO

Star Trek

THE FIRST SEASON

If you drive south along Gower from Hollywood Boulevard, across Sunset, and then toward Melrose Avenue, you quickly pass a set of blocklike television and movie studio buildings with tiny doors that open out onto the street. During the day you'll see lines of people at the entrances, waiting for tickets to see the taping of America's most popular shows. Then, suddenly, you pass a studio gate. It's the Gower Gate entrance to Paramount. Then you come to the intersection of Gower and Melrose. If you make a left and drive another half block, you'll come upon the entrance to Paramount Pictures. In 1965, however, when the second Star Trek pilot, "Where No Man Has Gone Before," was purchased by NBC, the Gower Gate entrance to Paramount was actually the main gate entrance to Desilu Studios, the home of Star Trek. Desilu and Paramount were back to back, separated from one another by a single wall. And it was at the Desilu Gower Street facilities where the original series was scheduled to be filmed once Gene Roddenberry and Desilu had received the green light from NBC to begin production.

Both "The Cage" and "Where No Man Has Gone Before" had been filmed at Desilu's Culver City studios, south and west of Hollywood, a good forty-minute drive in traffic. Now, with the start-up of the first twenty-six episodes of the original series, the *Star Trek* production facilities were to be moved from Culver City to Sound Stages 8 and 9 at Desilu's Gower Street studios. With only a six-month window to relocate the entire production and transform the company that had shot two pilots into a company capable of completing a new episode

The male stars complained that the haircuts might be fine for warping through deep space in the twenty-third century, but they looked downright odd for a Saturday-night pot of chili at Chasens.

every six days for twenty-six weeks, Roddenberry had to move quickly.

At the same time, Gene Roddenberry also updated the series's bible, rewriting characters to reflect the needs of an ongoing series. And the ship's doctor role underwent a change with the appearance of DeForest Kelley as Dr. Leonard McCoy, a crusty country doctor who was almost a re-creation of the role he had played as the police crime lab chief in the pilot for *Police Story*.

Bob Justman, though officially the associate producer, took on more and more of the production responsibilities as Roddenberry focused on the stories and scripts for the first season's episodes. In addition to hiring the production crew, he recruited Matt Jefferies as the set designer, Costume Designer William Ware Theiss, and makeup artist Fred Phillips as the head of the makeup department. It would now become Phillips's job not only to maintain the look of Mr. Spock and the rest of the crew, but to come up with new designs for alien life-forms for each weekly episode.

Interestingly enough, one of the first problems Phillips faced as the head of makeup was the design of the men's haircuts. Roddenberry had insisted that the men wear hairstyles that gave them a futuristic look, a look that was still undefined but was definitely not the way most men styled their hair in the middle 1960s. The male stars complained that the hair-cuts might be fine for warping through deep space in the twenty-third century, but they looked downright odd for a Saturday-night pot of chili at Chasens. How to resolve this problem? The answer was actually staring them in the face all the time: all the men's sideburns would have the same shape as Mr. Spock's. In a memo, Roddenberry wrote:

Per conversations with most concerned, the problem of too modern hairstyles on male actors in "Star Trek," regulars as well as both SAG and SEG, has been resolved. Rather than requesting altering of the basic contour favored by the actor, a simple and easily adjustable change is being made into the sideburns, i.e. pointing the bottom of them rather than wearing them square across.

For those doing single jobs on our show, it is easily adjustable via hair growth in a few days, or touching with a makeup pencil, actual shaving unnecessary. Where possible, however, even on such extras, we would prefer the proper job.

This is mandatory for all actors appearing in our show.

For Dr. McCoy, Roddenberry wrote Bob Justman:

> *Regarding Deforest Kelley's haircut for the "Star Trek" series, I would prefer that it be the same style that he had in the "Police Story" pilot, with the additional specification that the sideburns come to a point.*
>
> *Can you come up with a couple of photos from "Police Story" pilot which show Dee's hair style clearly so his barber will be able to recreate it? Thank you.*

MICHAEL WESTMORE

One of the reasons the episodes on the original series seemed so brightly colored as opposed to the muted colors on *The Next Generation* was that the show had to be able to play over black-and-white television sets. While color broadcasting had officially taken over television in 1965, the majority of sets in people's homes were still black-and-white, which, from a makeup artist's standpoint, meant that the colors, tones, and hues you chose had to be translated into black-and-white contrast. Many times, it wasn't the actual color of an actor's skin makeup that was important but the intensity or registration of the color. This explains why the different races were as deeply toned as they were and why the contrast between Bele and Lokai was represented by black and white. If we redid "Let That Be Your Last Battlefield" for today's broadcast technology, we'd probably use something other than black and white.

THE MAKING OF SPOCK

By late May 1966, the cast and creative personnel were all in place, with Jack Stone hired to assist Fred Phillips with makeup and Virginia Darcy in charge of hairstyles. And on May 24, 1966, filming of episode 1, "The Corbomite Maneuver," began at the Desilu Gower Street Studios. Leonard Nimoy reported in at 6:30 A.M. for his makeup call. Fred had already arrived fifteen minutes earlier and had laid out a new set of foam latex Spock ears along with other supplies and tools at his makeup station. A little after 6:30, Leonard Nimoy settled himself into Fred's makeup chair and gave his breakfast order to the production assistant who popped his head in to take orders over to the studio commissary. Then, Leonard settled into the chair and the transformation began.

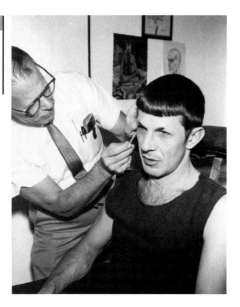

Step 1

Fred swabbed down Leonard's ears with a little rubbing alcohol to wash away any oil. If any light hair had grown on the ear, Fred trimmed it away.

Step 2

Fred slipped the Spock ear appliance over the top of Leonard's cleaned and trimmed ear, checking not only for fit and placement, but also to make sure it was pointed at exactly the correct angle. Now satisfied, Fred brushed a thin layer of adhesive called spirit gum over the ear, slipping the ear appliance in place. Then he repeated the entire process for the other ear.

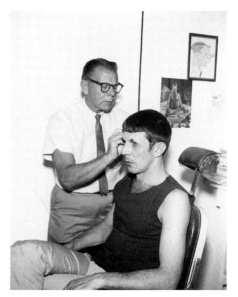

Step 3

Leonard's ears were still sticking out too far from his head, giving him an almost comical appearance. So, as he did in "The Cage," Fred pressed a small section of double-sided toupee tape behind each ear. Then he peeled off the wax paper backing and gently pressed Leonard's upper ears against the clear plastic adhesive strips, holding the ears close against the sides of Leonard's head. At about the this time, the production assistant would usually appear in the makeup room with Leonard's typical breakfast, a bacon and egg sandwich with a thick slice of onion. And as Leonard ate, the makeup work continued.

Step 4

Fred brushed a thin layer of plastic sealer over the edges of the appliance ears and then slightly onto Leonard's real ear so as to seal the edge of the foam pieces and keep them from shifting color. Fred then brushed a yellowish-tinged shade of Max Factor's Rubber Mask Greasepaint, known in the film makeup industry as R.M.G., onto the appliance and then over the rest of the ear, blended off, and then lightly powdered. This shade, called "Chinese," gave the character's skin a warm hue and vibrancy under the lights on the set, and further set Spock off from the other members of the *Enterprise* bridge crew.

Step 5

Fred applied a cream base in the exact same color of the greasepaint to the rest of Leonard's face and neck, blending in highlights and shadows to impart a third dimension to Spock's look. Then Fred dusted Leonard's face and neck with a translucent powder to blend the color and give off additional luster. Through the camera lens, this gave the character an intensity and highlighted its alien features.

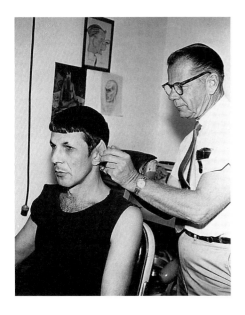

Step 6

Fred applied a gray-blue eye shadow to Leonard's eyelids.

Step 7

Fred sketched the extension of Spock's eyebrows with a makeup pencil. Working away from the tuft of Leonard's remaining real eyebrow, he painted spirit gum over these sketches and worked short lengths of yak hair, blended with Leonard's own hair color, into the adhesive.

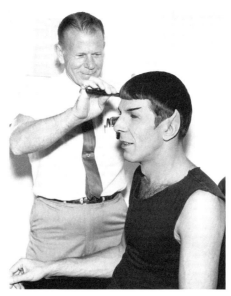

Photos this page courtesy of Stephen Poe

Step 8

In the final step, Fred blended a Max Factor pancake makeup over Leonard's hands so they matched his face. And in under two hours, Fred had transformed Leonard into what has become one of television's most enduring and intriguing characters.

Mr. Spock's looks were still a strong concern for NBC executives even before they aired the first episode of *Star Trek* in fall 1966. They worried that their local affiliates would receive protests complaining about the pointed-eared satanic look of the character. Inside the official press kit for the show was a shot of Spock at his

science station console. But the shot was not the Spock that ultimately appeared on television screens. This Spock had rounded ears with the tips bobbed away and the slanted eyebrows airbrushed out so they looked perfectly normal. Nobody protested in advance of the show, and the first aired episode, "The Corbomite Maneuver," starring film director Ron Howard's younger brother Clint as Balok, launched the series.

BALOK

There were actually two memorable alien characters in this episode, one the alter ego of the other. Balok himself was a childlike creature testing the self-proclaimed peaceful motives of the Starfleet crew. The Balok puppet, a frightening huge head that worked just like a ventriloquist's dummy, was simply a prop created by master designer Wah Ming Chang.

Balok was conceived as an inexpensively made up alien that was created by gluing a premade John Chambers plastic bald cap around Clint Howard's hairline with spirit gum. Once dry, the edges of the cap were dissolved by using a small amount of acetone so that the seam between the cap and the actor's head would be invisible on camera. The overall skin tone was established by sponging a tan cream base over Clint Howard's bald cap and face. As a final touch, hand-laid bushy eyebrows were glued into place, almost belying the childlike look of the alien. This was an effective use of makeup

because it was just bizarre enough to create a contrast between the *Enterprise* crew and the alien, but was completely nonthreatening in contrast to the menacing dummy Balok used to instill fear.

Wah Chang's puppet, reminiscent of his creations for *The Outer Limits*, was a very inventive use of a stage prop as a character. Nothing is more basic and recognizable than a ventriloquist's dummy, a mainstay of 1950s television, with its fixed stare and movable lower lip and chin. As it appeared, framed by the *Enterprise*'s forward viewscreen, the lightbulb-shaped head, forlorn but impassive expression,

Opposite:
The "real" Balok.

almost empty eyes, and long nose completely dominated the attention of the audience as it threatened to destroy the *Enterprise.* Ultimately, the appearance of the Munchkinlike Balok explained another function of the prop: that fear, especially fear of the unknown, is the most destructive of all forces.

THE SALT CREATURE

Wah Chang's salt-eating creature, the beast who figured so prominently in the episode "The Man Trap," is the last inhabitant of planet M-113. The salt creature isn't a monster, however; it's a sentient life-form whose relationship with its provider has been upset by the arrival of the *Enterprise,* and that's what triggers its killing spree. Accordingly, Wah Chang's design of the creature conveyed the aspects of its loneliness and desperation,

which were prominently displayed by its haunting expression. It was an angst-ridden creature whose equilibrium had been upset and which was killing to protect its only source of sustenance. Chang was able to convey the visual impression of all of this in his design. Wah himself said that he wanted to give the salt creature an emotional dimension so that it would be perceived as a life-form with its own validity. The creature was trapped in a symbiotic relationship that it had to protect in order to stay alive, and its eyes bespoke more doleful sadness than violence.

The creature's features were first sculpted out of modeling clay, and then a plaster mold was lifted off the sculpture and filled with liquid latex. After drying overnight, the cured latex mask was then peeled out in one piece and painted.

Then Wah attached a white wig to the mask, affixed glass alien-looking lenses for eyes, and, once the whole appliance was fitted over actress Sharon Gimpel's head, cut eye slits into the creature's wrinkles so Sharon could see where she was going. The slits also acted as air vents. For her hands, Wah fabricated a pair of slip-on gloves with suction-cut tentacles for fingers.

The alien makeup appliances were enhanced by William Theiss's costume, which was made out of a fur bodysuit that bulked up the actress so she looked more formidable.

RUK

A towering, menacing android that guards Captain Kirk after he and Nurse Chapel beam down to the planet Exo III

to visit exobiologist Roger Korby, Chapel's former fiancé, Ruk was the creation of Fred Phillips. To create the frightening android, Fred slipped a plastic bald cap over actor Ted Cassidy's head, covering his hair, and glued down the edges of the cap with spirit gum. Then Fred mixed a pale base color of grease-paint and spread it evenly over the cap and the actor's face and neck. Using a darker color, Fred painted strong shadow features under the cheekbones and beneath the eyes to give Ted's character a skull-like look that enhanced the already strong features of the actor's face. The area beneath his eyes was darkened even further to give him a sunken, hollow-eyed look that reinforced the lonely, haunted nature of the android.

...the network recommended that the visuals be toned down so as not to shock and offend viewers.

"MIRI"

This particularly chilling episode featured Kirk being kicked and beaten by a group of children who are the living guinea pigs in a experiment to prolong life. The adults of the planet died gruesome deaths; the children, though centuries old, are the last remaining inhabitants and mistrust all adults. The makeup and effects were so powerful in the original script that the network's Broadcast Standards Department recommended that the visuals be toned down so as not to shock and offend viewers. In particular, they recommended that the blemishes, so prominent on the inhabitants, be restrained and that the amount of blood during the fight scenes be decreased. They were particularly worried about the scene in which Kirk is beaten by the children, because of its brutality. But the "Miri" episode is also important because during the final scene, when McCoy develops an antidote to the drug and uses it on himself, the same kind of stop-action photography used in "The Cage" is used here in reverse to show the gradual disappearance of McCoy's blotches and blemish marks.

"THE MENAGERIE"
CHRISTOPHER PIKE

Because of the accelerated production schedule and the speed with which the show ate up new scripts, Roddenberry and Justman very quickly found themselves fresh out of material they could shoot. Scripts were in development, but the show was looking for some breathing room. Bob Justman suggested that they find a way to repackage what they had already shot in the original pilot. They just had to work the pilot into the series and they would buy themselves more time to bring scripts that were already in the pipeline into preproduction.

As the only common denominator between the pilot and the episodes was the character Spock, they could write an "envelope" that could wrap around the pilot and tie it into the series. Roddenberry rewrote the script, renaming it "The Menagerie," the original title of the pilot before "The Cage."

Makeup, and the use of the wheelchair prop with its "Yes/No" blinking light, played the critical roles in the "The Menagerie," using the effects to camouflage the fact that another actor would be playing Pike. The new Pike would only have to look vaguely similar to the original Pike. Because the story called for Pike to be confined into a twenty-third-century wheelchair and so permanently injured that he would not be able to speak, there was some latitude in casting the new Pike. They picked actor Sean Kenney.

Casting director Joe D'Agosta had first noticed how strong the resemblance was between Sean Kenney and Hunter, but Roddenberry had to explain to Kenney that his hair would be dyed a stark white and he would be wearing extensive latex makeup that would so inhibit his movements that he would probably have to eat through a straw. Did he have a problem with being confined within a tight space

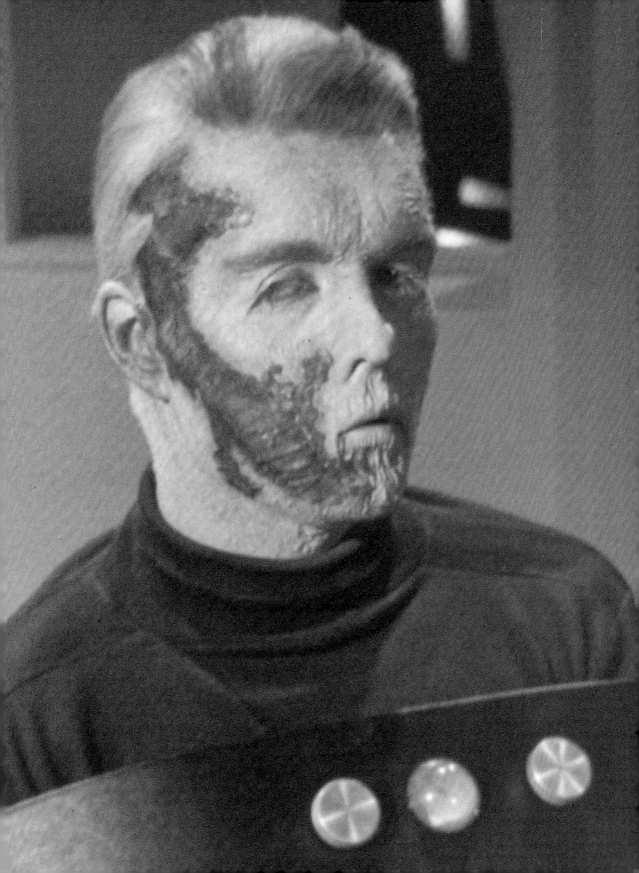

for long periods of time? Sean Kenney said he'd be honored to play the role of Captain Christopher Pike.

Fred Phillips began by making a life mask of Kenney's face to use as a makeup-testing device while hairstylist Virginia Darcy went to work on Sean's hair. Roddenberry wanted it brittle and white—not just streaked with temporary makeup, but dyed so white that it made the whole character look damaged as well as aged. After Virginia finished, they walked the actor down to the set for testing under the lights. Not surprisingly, Sean's hair color was so bright, it was off the color band and made the television signal almost crackle. It was deemed too "hot" for the lights, and had to be deepened. Virginia fixed this by mixing a beige powder with a hair preparation and combing this through Sean's hair and allowing it to dry. Once that was done, the hair color passed the color registration test and Sean was moved to the next stage of makeup tests.

Two days prior to shooting, Fred Phillips and makeup artist Ray Sebastian began camera tests on the designs they'd come up with using Sean's life mask. Now it was time to apply them for real and test them on camera, a six-and-a-half-hour application process. Ray Sebastian, not Fred, was in charge of the application process and was assisted by Jack Obringer.

The disfigurement/age makeup was constructed directly on Kenney's own skin instead of using latex appliances. The process began with the application of spirit gum all over Sean's face to create a tacky surface on the skin, which was then covered with cotton. The excess cotton was removed. Then liquid latex was stippled onto different sections of Sean's face while the skin was stretched tightly. They were working against the clock during the whole process, so instead of waiting for the latex to dry naturally, they used hair

dryers to speed up the drying time. Then they applied a second layer of latex.

Originally the scar on the side of Pike's face was a real problem to create during the test makeups on the Kenney mask. Finally, they decided to use denim fabric, which was cut out and attached to the right side of Sean's face. Then a base color of Rubber Mask Greasepaint was applied, covering Sean's entire face except for the scar. Then the scar was colored with a bluish-purple center and a deep red outer area to make it look perpetually sore. The entire makeup was set with a translucent face powder. Pike's eye, however, was given special treatment, because during tests the makeup designers realized that the character would look more sympathetic if he had a drooping eyelid. Therefore, Ray Sebastian used clear medical tape to pull down the outer edge of Sean's eyelid.

Sean remembers that the process was painstaking and tedious because it had to be re-created from scratch each time over the course of five days of shooting. He just about lived in the makeup room, he said, spending ten to twelve hours in there each day of the shoot. Then, he was strapped into position in an actual wheelchair that was motorized and outfitted with an outer plastic shell. Although Pike was supposed to be paralyzed, Sean himself maneuvered the wheelchair and worked the light.

ROMULANS

Star Trek in its thirty-five-year history has not only created some of television's most enduring icons and emblems but has actually helped humanity conceive of the way extraterrestrial alien cultures could evolve. In addition to the Vulcans, the Romulans and the Klingons stand out as two of the most enduring alien species in the whole history of television. The Romulans were the next recurring aliens

Romulans, first cousins to the Vulcans, have a similar physical appearance...because they shared many of the makeup characteristics of Spock, they were too expensive to bring back on a regular basis.

to be introduced to the world of *Star Trek*. They were the first true adversaries the crew of the *Enterprise* would be pitted against, in "Balance of Terror."

Romulans, first cousins to the Vulcans, have a similar physical appearance. Accordingly, during the original series, because they shared many of the makeup characteristics of Spock they were too expensive to bring back on a regular basis. Not only was the cost of manufacturing latex ears too great for multiple actors in each episode, but the manpower required to apply the latex and create the ears for each individual actor would have stretched the below-the-line costs beyond the budget. Therefore many background Romulans wore helmets, which could be reused, removing the need of creating expensive actor-specific ears. The job of manufacturing the Romulan helmets fell to Wah Chang, who

Michael Ansara and Susan Howard as Klingons.

built them out of liquid latex rubber to which he added a clay filler that made the finished pieces rigid. Wah's process was much cheaper than using conventional fiberglass or formed metal. Cost was clearly a factor here, according to Chang, but because the Romulan helmets were slip-cast, one helmet could fit many different actors. Therefore, even the more physically expensive helmets wound up saving money, while at the same time they gave the Romulans a distinctive look and were used again in "Amok Time" and "The *Enterprise* Incident."

KLINGONS

First established in "Errand of Mercy," the Klingons have become one of the most popular alien cultures on *Star Trek*. They've evolved considerably over thirty-five years, from the dark-skinned bushy-eyebrowed humanoids of John Colicos and Michael Ansara to the thick bones and overpowering presence of Christopher Lloyd in the *Star Trek* feature film and, ultimately, Michael Dorn and the Klingons on *Deep Space Nine*. Gene L. Coon, who wrote "Errand of Mercy," not only helped create the Klingons, but also defined the premise for a hostile, warlike race. From a makeup standpoint in the original series, Klingons were easy to create. A dark brown cream base was applied to the actors' faces, giving them a swarthy look. Lace mustaches and goatees were glued on using spirit gum, and the eyebrows were enhanced and thickened to make them appear bushy. Without extensive makeup appliances or any other grotesque features, Klingons could be made up easily and appear in groups. It wouldn't be until *Star Trek: The Motion Picture* and advances in the kind of devices available to makeup artists that the Klingons would undergo a fundamental design change. Although the Romulans were introduced first into the *Star Trek* universe as the ongoing villains, the makeup procedures were too costly to maintain. Accordingly, the Klingons, much cheaper to create, replaced the Romulans.

THE GORN

Wah Ming Chang created one of his most famous monster aliens of all time, the reptile Gorn, for the episode "Arena." Captain Kirk is pitted against a powerful bipedal reptile with menacing glowing eyes in a battle to the death arranged by the Metrons.

The Gorn had to be a mobile creature, a sculpted costume built out of props, which made it far more than a simple makeup job. The Gorn would be inhabited by a stuntman—Bobby Clark and Gary Coombs alternated in the role—who not only had to be able to utilize weapons and struggle with Kirk, but also had to be able to see through the monstrous eyes. The Gorn suit was constructed in sections so that the stuntman could slip in and out of it easily. Also, whenever only a portion of the Gorn was needed for a shot, they could use just a portion of the suit. That was why, Wah explained, he also sculpted the glove very carefully, because the script called for a closeup of the Gorn's hand picking up a rock.

Wah sculpted the head, hands, and feet using modeling clay on plaster positives. He then made a two-piece plaster mold of each sculpture. The final pieces were made of slush liquid latex, which had been poured into each of the negative molds. Once the latex was dry, the pieces were peeled out and painted using a mixture of rubber cement, colorant, and thinner that Wah air-brushed on.

The Gorn's body was constructed out of a neoprene diving suit jacket. Wah cemented poly-foam buildups for the arms and chest on the jacket. Because the wet suit jacket was meant to keep divers warm on the inside even in cold water, he cut a series of holes into the jacket to allow for more ventilation. Similarly, the legs were constructed over a pair of diving pants, and then the jacket and pants were painted to match the other pieces. The problem with seam lines between the different sections of the suit was solved by William Ware Theiss, who outfitted the Gorn's tunic and gauntlets. Finally, Wah painted the eyes a dark brown, but has said that, unbeknownst to him, someone changed them to look like

reflective lenses, giving the Gorn more of a shiny, reptilian look.

MICHAEL WESTMORE ON THE GORN

The difference between a character like the Gorn and one like the Hirogen from *Voyager* is a difference in makeup technology over thirty or so years. For all his mobility in Wah's costume and props, the Gorn, because of the heavy rubber appliances and the thick wet suit, is relatively slow and cumbersome. In contrast, the Hirogen are far more mobile, because unlike the Gorn's wet suit the Hirogen did not wear a full bodysuit. This gave the actors far more mobility, which is why the very overpowering Hirogen in *Voyager* move more easily and can do more in a scene than the lumbering Gorn, even though the Gorn was a very advanced creation for his time.

THE HORTA

The Horta, the star of "The Devil in the Dark," was actually the inspiration for writer Gene L. Coon's story. Coon saw the Horta first, a creation of stuntman/creature-builder Janos Prohaska, who walked by the *Star Trek* production offices carrying what looked like a big glob of gook with a raised center and a fringe around the outer edge. Seeing Gene Coon, Prohaska dropped to the cement pavement, crawled into the creature costume he was dragging along, and started to perform. He had even rigged a prop gimmick that would allow the creature to lay an egg, and during the demonstration for Coon, he plopped an egg out of the costume right there on the Desilu lot. Gene Coon stood there, so captivated by the creature squirming on the ground in front of him that he wrote the script "The Devil in the Dark," featuring a sympathetic alien who only wanted to protect her young from miners threatening their existence.

THE NEURAL PARASITES

These props as characters were fabricated out of translucent hot melt vinyl and were able to "breathe" by means of a small balloon that had been inserted into the center membrane. Like the ones used for the pulsating temple veins on the Talosians, the balloon bladders were supplied with air through long, flexible tubing that ran to a rubber bulb. Squeeze the bulb and the balloon bladder inflated; release it and it deflated. To create one of the episode's most dramatic effects, the melting and dissolving of the parasites under the UV rays of the sun, Prop Master Irving A. Feinberg had special dummy parasites created out of pure wax. When the time came for them to die, one of the crew aimed a powerful heat gun at the wax prop and it melted on camera.

THE EVOLUTION OF SPOCK

All during the first season, Spock's makeup continued to evolve, going through ever-so-slight transitions as Fred Phillips continued to experiment. Early in the season, for example, Fred started using just a hint of blush on Leonard's cheeks to give Spock a look of intensity and color. He also left Leonard's face a bit shiny under the lights, as he did with the other men on the set. But as Fred watched the dailies and evaluated his makeup work, he decided he didn't like the blush on Spock. So he eliminated it entirely and in its place applied a light dusting of dry greenish eyeshadow. This tended to cool his look down without a loss of intensity. Also, Fred eliminated the shiny finish to Spock's face, because, as the lore of the Vulcan homeworld evolved, Spock had to look cool instead of hot. It made sense because Vulcan was a hot and arid world, devoid of moisture in the atmosphere. Therefore, Fred decided that Vulcans should never look moist or sweaty, always displaying a flat matte finish. The matte finish of the Vulcan complexion became a character trait that lasted through all incarnations of *Star Trek* and is still a feature of Tuvok on *Voyager*.

of the most popular characters, was scheduled to lead off the second season in an episode called "Amok Time." A character named Chekov, portrayed by Walter Koenig, was added to the cast to appeal to teenage viewers. Hairstylist Pat Westmore, of the famed Westmore makeup dynasty, took over from Virginia Darcy, who stepped down as department head.

Leonard Nimoy and Arlene Martel in "Amok Time."

THE SECOND SEASON

The first season of *Star Trek* was plagued by poor Nielsen ratings and was considered such a dud by NBC that it was in real danger of cancellation. But loyal fans deluged NBC with a letter-writing campaign that encouraged the executives to change their minds. The network purchased a second season's worth of episodes. Spock, who had become one

In "Amok Time," Fred Phillips returned to Spock's shiny blushed complexion to establish the difference between the logical, in-control Spock and Spock overwhelmed by his biological imperative to mate. As Spock's mood became more intense, Phillips underscored it visually with starker highlights and an increasingly sweaty complexion leading up to the climactic hand-to-hand combat with Kirk. When the spell is broken and Spock is back on board the *Enterprise,* his makeup has returned to a flat, dry, matte look that represents his return to his former self.

THE FEEDERS OF VAAL

Working with many bare-chested extras in the episode "The Apple" required Fred Phillips to hire a whole crew of hairstylists and body-makeup artists to provide the humanoids of Gamma Trianguli VI their common characteristics of white hair, an orange-tan skin complexion, and painted designs on their faces. The leader of the humanoids, Akuta, also had antennae, so that he could receive commands from their perceived deity, Vaal.

To start the process each morning, the hairdressers would pin-curl the actor's hair, piling it on top of his or her head, after which they placed a nylon wig cap over the hair. Then the actor moved to the next station, where a makeup artist

applied orange-tan cream base, covering the actor's entire face and neck. A white cream liner was then applied under each eye, which was pulled up to form a sharp point. This procedure was carried out on both men and women. The artist then drew, freehand, an alien design on the sides of the actor's face, and then the entire makeup application was set using a translucent face powder. A bit of white cream liner was also added to the eyebrows so they would match the wig. Then it was on to the next station, where the body makeup was applied.

At the body-makeup station, the makeup artist blended the different colors of Max Factor Liquid Body Makeup so that it matched the color used on the face and neck. Using a damp natural sea sponge, the artist worked the color section by section over the body. Great care had to be taken so that there were no streaks or blotches and that the body makeup looked completely even. Then it was back to the hairstylist's station.

The hairstylist applied and adjusted the wig and then pushed hairpins through the

wig's foundation and into the wig cap to anchor it and keep the whole apparatus in place. Doing this properly was especially important, because if the wig flew off during a stunt, the entire scene would have to be reshot, an especially expensive process for this episode because of the number of extras and the amount of budget allocated to makeup and hairstyling. The makeup people and hairstylists were on the set during all the "feeder"

takes to make constant touch-ups during the shooting. After lunch, the actors and extras were marched back to the makeup, hair, and body-makeup tables so that everything, especially the wigs, could be checked for any needed repairs.

THE ANDORIANS AND TELLARITES

In "Journey to Babel," Mark Lenard, the Romulan commander from the first season, debuted in what would become his continuing role as Spock's father, Ambassador Sarek. Television legend Jane Wyatt also made her first appearance as Spock's mother, Amanda. In this episode, the two lead aliens, the Tellarites and the Andorians, have strikingly different appearances, a makeup feat in itself given the tight budget of the show and the need to have another set of Vulcan ears for Marc Lenard.

The Tellarites have snouts, hooded eyes, bushy eyebrows, and facial hair. They look uncomfortably like pigs. Gav, the Tellarite ambassador, played by John Wheeler, wore makeup that consisted primarily of a one-piece foam latex appliance that covered the central part of his face. The piece was glued on in such a way that the actor's eyes could hardly be seen, and, as a result, John Wheeler could barely see where he was going. Just like Gary Lockwood in "Where No Man Has Gone Before," Wheeler had to tilt his back while he was delivering his lines in order to see through his makeup appliance. It was this tilt that gave the impression of Gav's being aloof and superior, and added immeasurably to Wheeler's performance, even though he never intended to do it at first. In order to complete Gav's makeup, a beard and mustache were hand-laid to blend off into the rest of his hair. The mustache helped to conceal the edge of the snout appliance and formed

an interesting effect with the character's bushy eyebrows. Gav's look was topped off with character gloves.

The Andorians were a striking blue color, setting them off from the rest of the *Enterprise*'s diplomatic guests, and had bright white hair with two antennae protruding through. Fred Phillips had sculpted the antennae using modeling clay. According to *Star Trek* archivist Richard Arnold, Fred had used the ends of thread spools for the tips of the Andorians' antennae, whose main stems were made of a rigid material and attached to the white wigs. The blue makeup was Max Factor Aqua Blue cream stick with a slightly deeper blue cream liner to shadow the face.

OLD AGE MAKEUP IN "THE DEADLY YEARS"

When you realize that makeup department heads and prop masters are sometimes the last people to see what's called for in a new script, you can almost picture the shock on Fred Phillips's face when he read the first draft of the script for "The Deadly Years," which described not just one set of age makeup, but five. Four of the old-age makeups were on the series regulars, and, to make matters even more difficult, the actors had to be seen getting progressively older during the course of the show.

Even under normal conditions, old-age makeup was a tremendous challenge to pull off because of the time constraints it placed on the makeup artist running a weekly show. The success or failure of any makeup depends largely on the amount of lead time the makeup artist is given. On *Star Trek* during the second season, two weeks was a normal lead time, but this type of makeup job would have normally demanded four to six weeks of prep because of the experimentation required for the aging process, especially on the characters of Kirk and McCoy. Fred had eleven days to prepare.

Already behind schedule, Fred put out urgent calls to his regular day-checkers to corral whomever was available to help with this episode. He ended up having Jack Petty gaffing (coordinate) the show and hired Don Cash, Thomas Tuttle, Kiva Hoffman, Lester Bernes, Hal King, Ellis L. Burman, and James Phillips. The artists began making molds they could use to create the necessary appliances. What they couldn't fabricate themselves they tried to purchase by calling around to find such generic appliances as eye bags and standardized wrinkles. These were used with the molds to begin the prepping process. Then the first stage of the makeup was completed by using as many conventional techniques as possible, such as highlights and shadows to project an aging effect on camera.

For stage two of the makeups, the artists used a process known as stretch and stipple, wherein the artist stretches the area under the actor's eyes and applies liquid latex. A hair dryer was used

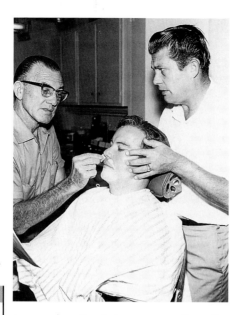

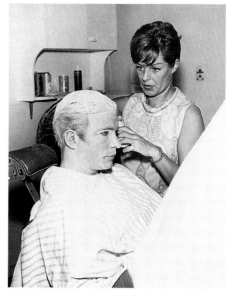

At left, Paul Malcolm applies makeup, while Jack Petty stretches Shatner's face to help create wrinkles.

Right: Pat Westmore adds some final touches.

Photos this page courtesy of Stephen Poe

to speed up the drying process. Once the skin was dry, it was released and, because of the latex, bunched up and created realistic wrinkles. The rest of the face was then made up using highlights and shadows. At this stage as well, hairstylist Pat Westmore brushed a liquid graying compound through the actor's hair to give the appearance of graying at the temples. The same type of graying was used to age the eyebrows. At each stage, the hair and eyebrows continued to be dyed increasingly gray to show how the artificial aging process advanced during the episode.

In stage three of the process, the makeup artists performed more stretch and stipple on the actors to cover more of their faces. Some actors received additional layers of latex to give the illusion of deeper wrinkles and more sag. Where Fred wanted to see a loss of hair and advancing baldness, actors wore special wigs in addition to receiving additional graying at the temples and eyebrows. Also at stage three the tops of the actors' hands were stretched and stippled to show wrinkling and aging of the skin.

At stage four, the actors had reached the extremes of aging, and the makeup required the application of foam appliance jowls and eye bags. Also, the stretch-and-stipple liquid latex wrinkling process was now applied to the actors' entire faces where there were no other appliances. At this point, too, full ventilated wigs were applied to all the actors, with the exception of Spock, because Vulcans age slower than humans. Therefore, Spock suffered the least effects from the aging process even though his eyebrows were made to look shaggier with application of lace eyebrow appliances.

MICHAEL WESTMORE ON "THE DEADLY YEARS"

On *TNG*, we were faced with a number of "aging" shows in which we had two types of stories: gradual aging and the presentation of an already aged character. The toughest are the gradual aging shows because the makeup has to be designed to go on in stages. In both Patrick Stewart's case in "The Inner Light" and also for Diana Muldaur in "Unnatural Selection," we had to age the principal

actors very carefully, because not only was consistency over the multiple-day shoot important, but there was consistency throughout the gradual aging cycle. We were fortunate in *TNG* to be working with a more advanced technology in foam latex appliances and more comfortable adhesives, which allowed the actors greater freedom with their performances.

THE MUGATO

The legendary single-horned beast with the deadly venomous bite was created for "A Private Little War," by stuntman/designer Janos "The Horta" Prohaska out of an old ape suit he had used for another project. But for *Star Trek*, Janos attached a single horn to the top of the head and a set of protruding back spines. As he did in the Horta, Janos inhabited the mugato.

GALT, THE PROVIDERS, AND THE THRALLS

In "The Gamesters of Triskelion," it's the props that run the show: three ancient glass-enclosed brains in an underground chamber betting in quatloos on the outcome of gladiator-style combat. In reality, these brains were constructed out of hot metal vinyl, with air lines running through each brain to give the impression of pulsating, breathing life, and set inside cylinders along with colored lighting. The brains commanded a master of the drill thralls named Galt, played by Joseph Ruskin, who had a plastic bald cap glued to his head and was made up with a very pale cream. His eyes were then shadowed to make them look sunken and hollow.

Kirk's drill thrall, the exotic Shahna, was played by Angelique Pettyjohn, who looked, for all outward appearances, to be human. Dressed in a revealing William Ware Theiss costume, Shahna wore straight body makeup and a full, swept-back hairstyle created by Pat Westmore. Tamoon, Chekov's drill thrall, was made up in a fanciful colored base and body makeup and wore a wild hairstyle. Kloog, the thrall who eventually fought Kirk, had a tan complexion, dental appliances, and a beast-man hairstyle.

THE THIRD SEASON

The ratings for the second season were no better than they were for the first. In fact, they were so low that even before the end of the season, rumors were circulating around NBC that the show was due for imminent cancellation. It was only another letter-writing campaign and protest demonstrations outside NBC's Burbank studios that caused the network to give the show another season. But, everyone was quite sure, unless there was a turnaround in viewer numbers the third season could well be the last for *Star Trek.*

As if to underscore their displeasure with the show, the network cut the production budget. This, as it turned out, would not only stifle the creativity of the producers but would eliminate many of the location shoots, the larger-than-normal casts, and the use of many guest stars. There was a sharp constraint on the construction of new sets, and that meant that at least twenty-five percent of all the episodes had to be ship or "bottle" shows. Aliens would have to be simpler in their construction and design, and there would be a reduced use of prosthetics because of their high cost.

GORGAN

There were far fewer memorable aliens from the third season because of the constraints on the makeup staff, but among those who stand out are Melvin Belli's Gorgan, who becomes more and more horrific as the episode "And the Children Shall Lead" progresses. Although he appears as the "friendly angel" when summoned by the children, his avuncular appearance—shimmering white hair, happy large Santa Claus belly, and long flowing gown—actually belies his true nature. He is a monster. When the children no longer believe in him he is transformed into the monster in a process that Fred Phillips had used to age Susan Oliver in "The Cage." For each take of the decaying Gorgan, Fred applied one of a series of horrific makeups, and then put Belli back in front of the camera for the next few feet of footage. The result was a smooth transformation right before the eyes of the children of Triacus, who see the real Gorgan for the first time.

LOKAI AND BELE

Lokai and Bele, the black and white

Frank Gorshin as Bele.

fugitive and his white and black pursuer, respectively, became two of the standout aliens from the third season episode "Let That Be Your Last Battlefield." Maybe it was the performance of comedian Frank Gorshin or maybe it was the simplicity of the characters' makeup that carried so much meaning, but the episode is one of the most innovative productions of the series. For both actors, Lou Antonio as Lokai and Frank Gorshin as Bele, a length of masking tape was applied to the face to keep the color edge sharp and then the white makeup was applied. The makeup was set with baby powder. Then the masking tape was peeled off and the black makeup was applied to the other side of the face very carefully so as not to smudge the white. For a makeup department working on an impossibly tight budget, this was one of the cleverest ways to create aliens and save money at the same time.

SEVRIN

Much the same thinking about saving money went into the creation of Dr. Sevrin in "The Way to Eden." Played by veteran movie actor Skip Homeier, Dr. Sevrin sported large foam latex "cauliflower" ears, the staple plastic bald cap, and a painted flower design on his forehead. The alien nature of Sevrin's hippie followers was created with oddball hairstyles that defied even the conventions of a 1969 counterculture.

THE STANDOUT PROPS

Tribbles

Like the Providers, tribbles were one of the few props that actually became the stars of an episode. Tribbles were handmade by Wah Ming Chang out of artificial fur stuffed with foam plastic. For those tribbles that had to appear to move as if they were really alive, Wah inserted inflatable balloons operated by a squeeze mechanism. Still another tribble was able to twitch, because it was powered by a battery-powered toy dog sewn inside. Given the tight prep and shooting schedule for "The Trouble with Tribbles," Wah Chang's ability to hand-sew each tribble on the set turned out to be a near miracle.

The truth beneath a tribble.

Photos this page courtesy of the Gregory Jein Collection

Medical Equipment

One of the most interesting aspects of the high-tech medical equipment that proliferated in sickbay was the simplicity of the design. The tricorder was a Wah Ming Chang construction, but the odd shapes of metal on the medical consoles as well as those protruding from the clear plastic on the "Teacher's Helmet" in the "Spock's Brain" episode were simply pieces of metal machined into knob shapes and glued in place.

ALAN SIMS ON MEDICAL EQUIPMENT

One of the things that did not change over the years that separated the original series from *TNG, DS9,* and *Voyager,* is the prop master's challenge to create new props out of existing materials. Just as Wah Chang told me he did when assembling the hand communicators out of screening material and the buttons on the phaser out of typewriter keys, we used the same sort of approach when putting together the new one-piece flip-top tricorders for the *TNG* crew. The trick is to

"Props are...the art of compromise between what you want, what you think the producers want, and what you can actually get by the time shooting starts."

always keep your eyes open for anything that looks out-of-the-way and original that you think someday might make an interesting prop. You don't even need to know what prop you'll build, but if you have a storehouse of interesting-looking objects, you'll find a use for them. In the same way that Mike Westmore discovered the holographic object for Third of Five's eyepiece in *TNG*'s "I, Borg" when he was Christmas shopping one season, I look for something that I can say "that would make a great prop."

Props are also the art of compromise between what you want, what you think the producers want, and what you can actually get by the time shooting starts.

As hard as everyone had worked on the third year of *Star Trek*, the original series was canceled when the season came to an end in 1969. By the end of the third season of the original series, no one knew just how much a part of television history *Star Trek* would become.

CHAPTER THREE

Star Trek: The Next Generation

In October 1986, twenty years after the original series had first aired on NBC, Paramount announced the launch of Star Trek: The Next Generation. Star Trek had accumulated a lot of history, and its aliens and artifacts had become cultural icons. Through four motion pictures, the look of Star Trek had evolved, transmogrified from small-screen television to the overwhelming presence of the wide-screen movie theater. Now the challenge to the heads of makeup and props would be to take an established look and transform it back to television without losing any of the awe and fascination the Star Trek motion pictures had inspired.

MICHAEL WESTMORE

I came to *Star Trek: The Next Generation* from a long line of makeup artists. My grandfather, George Westmore, founded the first makeup studio in 1917 and brought each of his sons into the business. By the 1930s, all six of the Westmore brothers had become successful makeup artists with my father, Mont, working on the classic *Gone with the Wind* for David O. Selznick. But it was my uncle Bud, perhaps best known for his creation of

The Creature from the Black Lagoon at Universal Pictures, who ultimately brought me into the business, where I was trained by John Chambers.

My own career in feature films offered me some great opportunities to develop the skills that would later become crucial to the creation of aliens in *TNG*. When I worked on *Rocky*, for example, I had to manipulate the appliances during the climactic fight sequences, running back and forth between Sylvester Stallone and

In *Star Trek: First Contact*, Locutus's look from the series was integrated into the new makeup of the Borg created for the feature film.

Elliot Marks

Robbie Robinson

The producers figured that if most of their candidates told them they would use my lab maybe they should call me.

Carl Weathers to switch their makeup appliances as each fighter became more and more bloodied and bruised. Creating the increasingly battered Rocky Balboa was valuable training for my work in Martin Scorsese's *Raging Bull*, where I was responsible for changing the makeup appliance on Robert De Niro's face for every single scene of the film.

But in addition to my Academy Award–nominated *2010*, where I had to re-create Keir Dullea's makeup from the end of *2001: A Space Odyssey*, my other most successful Oscar-nominated feature films were *Clan of the Cave Bear*, *Star Trek: First*

Contact, and *Mask*, which won me an Oscar in 1985. All three of these films required heavy use of makeup effects and appliances to create the look of a different reality, no less credible than an everyday reality, but a reality that assumed an entirely different world.

When I decided to get away from doing movies around the world and stay at home, I found that the kind of work I did wasn't done on television. So I concentrated on developing makeup appliances in my studio for other makeup artists to use, the kinds of creative devices that would satisfy the demands of just about any type of character. And that was how my name was brought up to *TNG* producers Bob Justman and Rick Berman, who were interviewing makeup artists for the new series that was just starting production. Even though I hadn't been called in among the first round of candidates considered for the job, I was eventually contacted by the producers.

Bob and Rick had been interviewing many of my colleagues for the job of head of makeup, I had learned, and when they were asked what shop or lab they would use to provide their makeup appliances for aliens and other characters, most of them said they would use me. The producers figured that if most of their candidates told them they would use my lab maybe they should call me. So they did and asked me in for an interview.

I met with Bob Justman and Rick Berman and Unit Production Manager David Livingston and talked for a little over an hour about my work, the pictures I'd done, the challenges that the new *Star Trek* would present, the ideas I had for being able to come up with varieties of alien looks through the use of different types of appliances. Of course, we all understood the kinds of demands a *Star Trek* production could put on the facilities of a makeup department, and part of our conversation had to do with ways to absorb those demands and keep production schedule week after week no matter what the script called for. Aliens are sometimes easier to create on paper than they are in the makeup trailer. But part of the job was to make it look far easier than it truly was.

When the hour was just about up, I told them I had to leave. I had to meet Whoopi Goldberg, for whom I was making a dental appliance for one of her acts, and I didn't want to be late. Now that I wasn't doing feature films on a regular basis, keeping the shop and the lab

running and turning out jobs was important to me, so I needed to be very responsive to all my clients. But by the time I got home, there was a message on my answering machine. The producers said that if I wanted the job at *Star Trek*, it was mine. Please call back.

I called back right away and told them that I was indeed interested. But I wanted to think it over a little, I said. The job meant a long-term commitment, not doing any feature films, and staying put for a while. "You have an hour," they said, "because makeup tests start on Monday." So I talked it over with my wife, Marion, and we decided this was a great opportunity. I called the producers back and said, "Let's go." And that was how I became a part of *Star Trek: The Next Generation*, and the following Monday we began our makeup tests on Brent Spiner, who would play Data.

MICHAEL WESTMORE ON "THE PROCESS"

The process of creating new aliens, even from the first scripts that Roddenberry oversaw at the outset of *TNG*, was very straightforward. I was handed a script and told what the alien was, and the design was mostly left up to me. With the Klingons, I already had the basic design from the motion pictures. I added a Shakespearean style of facial hair and a forehead bone structure based on dinosaur vertebrae and I was able to modify motion picture Klingons for television. The Andy Probert design for the Ferengi was handed to me as well. I enhanced the look of the ears, which were too pointed, and shortened the length of the chin, added piranha-style teeth, and that was the look that has remained unchanged for thirteen years.

When I get an alien in a story, I have to work from the story. If the alien lives on a desert planet, I start with wondering what

The creation starts with an idea in clay.
Robbie Robinson

Once approved, molds are made of the actor's face, and the appliances are created.
Robbie Robinson

I enjoy basing my aliens on things we've seen here on Earth so they're recognizable. People watching the show can have a point of reference, and the alien has a meaning, rather than just a monster standing around that has no meaning for a television audience. If people are familiar with certain designs, maybe the shape and coloration of a butterfly wing or the shell of a turtle, it has a subconscious resonance that something completely unrecognizable won't have.

TNG would become a great challenge for me and for a lot of the design people because we had to build on a television and motion picture series that already had a look and a feel to it, but we couldn't really copy anything. It would have been easy just to duplicate what was already there and what the fans were accustomed to. But it would have become flat and boring very quickly. We, therefore, had to come up with something different that wouldn't be so much of a change that it would send fans away. That was the challenge.

We developed all of the characters into more realistic looks, from the Klingons to the Romulans, veterans from the original series. And we had to create new characters like the Ferengi. Part of the proof of our success was the two new series' spin-off characters we created for *TNG*.

EARLY MAKEUP CONCEPTS ON TNG

Because of televisions getting bigger, with higher resolution and better color, one of the first challenges the makeup team on *TNG* faced was to avoid creating a cartoon look for the aliens. Color broadcasting, the fad of the middle 1960s, was now standard fare in television, and as a result the makeup team couldn't simply rely on color to convey the otherworldly essence of its new aliens. They had to be

would someone look like who comes from a desert. I then research the environment on Earth rather than relying on science fiction magazines for inspiration. I start with the question, "What are we going to run into in the desert—snakes, lizards?" I use various books with illustrations that show me what comes from where. Then I organize all the different features of various types of animal life into files. I have a file on ears, a file on noses, one on teeth, or tails, or scaly skins that I can refer to to build an alien from a specific environment.

In the first year of TNG, everything was done the old-fashoned way, with greasepaint and sealer.

more innovative in their design, even when creating humanoid life-forms as strange as the Traveler.

Time constraints were also an issue and often limited the makeup department to working on an alien's head rather than coming up with bodysuits as appliances. Suits that transformed an alien's shape were so time-consuming, because they had to be custom-made, that even the Anticans and the Selay that the makeup department created were bipedal aliens rather than completely nonhumanoid. Suits on the original series were often made out of wet suits with scales on them. They weren't custom fabricated, and as a result they sometimes tended to look more like Halloween costumes than actual body shapes.

Contour became a design feature of TNG aliens. Oversized heads or a pronounced bone structure, an odd ear or skin marking, even teeth were changed. These were the subdued makeups created for the aliens the crew would meet. Thus the Klingons seemed to grow teeth in their transition from the motion pictures to The Next Generation. The new aliens called the Ferengi were immediately provided with rows of piranha teeth that seemed to sprout from their mouths as if they were the interlocking spines on a Venus's-flytrap. Because there were sometimes so many aliens filling a scene, it became important to define aliens by their silhouette rather than by the starkness of their color.

The art of makeup itself had advanced during the twenty years between the original series and TNG and provided makeup designers with new products, new types of foam latexes and appliances, and new bonding substances they could work with. In particular there was a new product called Pax, a combination of acrylic paint in a water-soluble medical glue and another type of silicone glue that had been developed for hospital use. Pax, for example, allowed the makeup artists to totally seal up an actor's face and do opaque colorings. This added a new dimension to the way a character's face could be designed and highlighted.

In the first year of TNG, everything was done the old-fashioned way, with greasepaint and sealer. Then the makeup department began working with Pax, because it covered the surface completely and didn't turn color during the course of a long day's shoot. It allowed the artists to create more subtle tones that would last under the hot lights and didn't have to be constantly retouched. Pax didn't absorb into the latex, which meant that the foam appliances had a longer life during a day's shoot. There was also an added benefit to using the new medical adhesives during the makeup application process: They were faster to use and lasted longer. That meant the makeup department could get the actor out faster, which translated into more time in front of the cameras than before, and the foam appliances could be saved for reuse. Not only was this a cost savings, but it allowed the makeup department to spend time on the design of new appliances instead of constantly refabricating existing appliances just to keep up with the pace of production.

During the first year, before they began using medical adhesives on the set, the makeup department would sometimes take a week to design a head appliance. After one day's shoot, the appliance might have to be completely rebuilt for the next day, because it would be destroyed in the removal process. After the use of medical adhesives was instituted, the appliance could be removed, and the makeup personnel could simply dry the appliance out and reuse it the next day. Even the most complicated appliances could be reused up to ten times. In fact, even today, the makeup department has Ferengi heads on the shelves that are twelve years old and, even though their edges might be crumbling, they're capable of being reused in a pinch.

The new types of foam appliances that had been developed between the original series and *TNG* were softer and gave the actors a greater mobility on the set. Since the makeup department was not relying on spirit gum as an adhesive—with its ether base the actors could feel very uncomfortable and it could even burn sensitive skin—they were able to create more elaborate appliances with medical adhesive, which was far more comfortable and didn't limit an actor's mobility. Medical adhesives evaporated quickly, unlike the older sealants, which sometimes trapped the ether fumes under the makeup and drove them through the surface of an actor's skin.

The use of less-irritating makeup also made it possible for producers to get a wider range of actors for the show. Many actors who previously simply didn't want to subject themselves to the discomfort of elaborate makeup appliances now found the roles easier to do because the makeup didn't bother them as much.

The new foam latex makeup appliances, rubber that was more flexible and doesn't tear easily, also meant that actors' movements didn't have to be constrained by the makeup. The older rubber tended to be stiff and had little natural movement. Now appliances are manufactured with plasticizers that give them much greater mobility and impart that mobility to the actors who wear them. Newer manufacturing methods mean that the smaller makeup appliances are so light, actors usually aren't even aware of them once shooting begins, and they don't interfere with a performance. Nowhere was this more apparent than in the design of the Klingons, where the *TNG* makeup department was able to create a more elaborate look, and yet not compromise the actors' mobility. A character once defined as an alien only by dark skin was turned into a completely sculpted nonhuman creature with well-defined bone structures, a fearsome set of teeth, and a striking hairstyle. Klingons could not only look menacing, but engage in hand-to-hand combat without fear of losing an appliance.

The Klingons from the original series were born out of the concept that the way to create an evil adversary was to paint his face dark brown and put a black wig on him and make him nasty and this is a Klingon. Then, as Klingons moved into the feature films, the makeup artists put a little ridge on the forehead. When the new makeup team for *TNG* was brought on, they took it a step further. Using Worf as their initial creation, they not only kept the ridges on the forehead, but enhanced them. They went heavier with the ridges so they would stand out in much greater relief. The bone structure was so pronounced and close to the surface of the skin that the Klingons evolved to a near-exoskeletal creature. It was clear that the Klingons were not just versions of

human, but definitely another race.

The design premise of the new Klingon foreheads in *TNG* was based on the look of prehistoric dinosaur vertebrae. By using dinosaur anatomy books, the makeup design could be created from just a small portion of a single vertebra. That accounts for the enormous variety of Klingon foreheads.

In addition, the makeup designers, wanting to accentuate more of the menacing otherworldliness of the Klingons, modified other facial features. They added a ridge to the nose that interlocks with the accentuated forehead bone structure, making it more fearsome. Changing the teeth became important, because now that the foreheads were enhanced and the nose structure was enlarged, it was suddenly evident that the Klingons had Hollywood white, perfectly straight teeth. The contrast between the

The Klingon Korrd (Charles Cooper) as seen in *Star Trek V.*
Bruce Birmelin

Above:
Charles B. Hyman as Konmel, sans Klingon teeth.

Right:
A whole new look for the Klingon race: Michael Dorn as Worf, as seen in this first-season publicity shot.

upper skull and face and mouth was suddenly overwhelming. Therefore, the make-up department started experimenting with creating acrylic yellow, snarly, craggy oversized teeth that were applied as caps directly over the actor's teeth. Michael Dorn was the first to wear the appliance. Thereafter, every speaking Klingon has worn upper acrylic teeth, saying his or her lines through a special set of caps fabricated for each actor and given to the actor two days in advance of shooting so he or she could get used to speaking through the appliance.

The motion pictures that were being shot during the same period as *TNG* featured an older version of the Klingons at first, with the subtle foreheads, and they were a little lighter in color. They had a "Palm Springs" tan rather than the deeper, darker colors of Worf and the Klingons on *TNG*, and the Klingons that were created for the feature film were based on the Worf design. In fact, the desire to create a more intense-looking Klingon from the ones in the early motion pictures had a simple explanation behind it: They had to look more alien.

Now that the look for Klingons was established, how to set Worf apart from the other Klingons? The Klingons favored long black hair, usually unkempt. Worf was different because he was a Starfleet officer and had to have more of a military bearing. Worf was given a tailored hairstyle, which set him off from the other Klingons.

MICHAEL WESTMORE

As I started sculpting the first forehead pieces for our Klingon guest stars, I was under the mistaken impression that each design had to be different for each actor. It was a time-consuming process, therefore, in the early seasons to create entirely new headpieces from scratch for each performer. The task of casting the actor's head, making a mold from it, and sculpting the elaborate bone structure generally takes about two days. This all changed for the episode "Redemption," which featured a large cast of Klingon characters. To save time, instead of making a separate cast for each actor's head, I would measure the head when the actor first walked into makeup and organize the "heads" according to size. If an actor's head came close to one of the preexisting molds, we'd create our new design on the mold that was closest in size to it.

If we had two actors with similarly sized heads, I would sculpt the first forehead design, and after taking a mold from it, the clay sculpture would still be intact. This would eliminate the need for putting clay on the mold. It was a real time-saver that allowed me to resculpt the second forehead in a matter of three hours instead of spending an entire day on a new sculpture. In crowd scenes, however, I try whenever possible to recycle the foreheads so that I don't have to spend time creating appliances when existing ones will work. This could backfire on me, though, when certain forehead designs that were too elaborate had to be retired from the show because they were so closely identified with a specific character, such as Kell in "The Mind's Eye." This also became an issue on *Deep Space Nine*, where the Klingon presence on the show was a constant, particularly in the later episodes.

After the forehead, teeth, and nose appliances are in place, it's time for the wigs. There were two basic types of wigs that we developed for the *Next Generation* Klingons. There were the basic, inexpensive, two-hundred-dollar wigs we used for the actors playing background Klingons and who were only involved for one or two days of shooting, and there were the

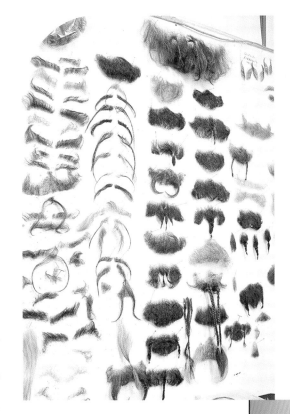

Robbie Robinson

wigs for the principal actors, such as Worf. For the background actors, we glued the wig directly to the headpiece on the first day after the makeup was in place. Then, after the day's shooting, when the actor's makeup was removed, we left the wig right on the headpiece, which we carefully lifted off the actor, taking special care not to disturb any of the structure. We cleaned off the edges of the forehead appliance extremely carefully, making sure there was no dried glue around the edges, so the piece could be reapplied the next day. Then, because the wigs were kept in place on the headpiece, they didn't have to be re-dressed for the next day's shooting. And that saved us lots of time and expense on the actors who were in the background and whose makeup wasn't required to stand up to any close-ups.

For Worf and any other principal Klingons, it was a whole different operation. First of

all, the wigs were made of hair lace, a far more expensive device that the hairstylist carefully glued in place right after the makeup was completed. Then Michael or one of the other principal Klingons was sent back to makeup, where we applied the mustache and beard. I really liked this part of the operation, because I was able to get real creative when it came to styling the facial hair.

Facial hair was one of my favorite operations with the Klingons because I was able to figure out great combinations of mustaches and beards that seemed to fit the different characters described in the scripts. Especially in the later episodes of *The Next Generation*, when Worf's brother Kurn and their rival Duras were stirring up the Empire and Gowron took the throne, I was able to work out family facial styles. By the way, I used as a model for the Klingons the facial hairstyles from the

Elizabethan period that I found in a book called *Fashions in Hair*.

In Gowron's case, we had a lot of fun by giving him nineteenth-century muttonchops down his face and connected with his mustache. For another Klingon, one that was especially antagonistic, I extended tips of his mustache all the way under his jawline and then brought them together into two points. That way they looked just like the pincers of a crab's claw. When he opened his mouth, the ends would separate. When he closed his mouth, they came together. In this way, the makeup was the effect itself, spooky, reinforcing the character and making everyone, especially the other actors, feel ill at ease whenever he was in a scene. This is how a facial-hair effect is supposed to work.

At the end of the day when Michael was finished shooting, the hairstylist removed the hair lace wig and blocked it by pinning it onto a head block. Then the stylist rolled curlers into it and re-dressed it for the next day's shoot. Every day that Michael or another principal Klingon was in a scene, we had to follow the same exact procedure so that in a complicated design not one piece of the makeup looked out of place when the film was edited into its final version.

As the Klingon story lines became more involved, especially after Worf and K'Ehleyr had a son, I began playing with ways to show family resemblances through similar forehead pieces. I wanted Alexander to have features that combined the full Klingon bloodlines of Worf and the half-Klingon background of K'Ehleyr, and this turned out to be a challenge. Suzie Plakson was very fair-skinned, and extraordinarily pretty. The makeup team didn't want to make her look like a barbaric Klingon woman with huge craggy teeth, so we decided to emphasize her humanity over her Klingon half by making her forehead structure more subtle, not giving her a nose piece, and keeping her skin light. But when it came to Alexander, I combined a smaller version of Michael's headpiece with a more subtle version of Michael's nose piece. However, I didn't touch his teeth, reflecting Suzie's look, and kept his skin lighter than Michael's by using a shade of brown for his makeup called ST-1. It's lighter than Michael but darker than Suzie.

Similarly, the Duras family and the terrible sisters Lursa and B'Etor had the same general forehead features as Duras. What worked for Duras and his sisters also had to work for Toral, Duras's son.

The other Klingon issues we had to manage during the years we filmed *The Next Generation* concerned designing a consistent look for all the different skin tones of the actors who played guest roles, such as John Tesh, who played one of the holodeck warriors in "The Icarus

Factor," and, of course, Suzie Plakson, who was in a number of episodes. Because we had a number of African-American actors who played Klingons as well as white actors, and because, among the African-American actors, there were a variety of skin tones, we had to come up with a way to define the Klingon look without over-making-up all the actors so they would have exactly the same skin tone; we had to come up with a design strategy. We settled on this strategy: all the natural brown-toned actors were Northern Klingons, like Worf. All the fair-

color with his headpiece. For the lighter tones, we used two shades of makeup, one of which was called Desert Tan and the other Malibu Tan, that deepened the color of the skin but allowed us to do a lot of shading and stippling to create grada-tions in color and color contours.

One of the most interesting and, for me, exciting devices I ever created for Klingons was Worf's vertebrae in "Ethics," the episode in which Worf suffered an injury that left him paralyzed and desperate for Will Riker to help him commit suicide. It was a truly intense performance for

Robbie Robinson

skinned actors were Southern Klingons. In that way, we were able to work with all the actors who portrayed Klingons regardless of their skin tones and without having to devise a median color for the makeup. For the Northern Klingon roles, we simply matched the actor's natural

Michael, who had to spend most of the episode flat on his back until he managed to struggle to his feet and walk upright at the end of the show. To objectify what it was that had failed, the script called for a depiction of the actual backbone of a Klingon. In a scene doctors removed

Worf's spine to repair it, so I had to build a spine, based on the actual length of Michael Dorn's real spine, that was composed of a large single vertebra for every two human vertebrae. And at the base of the spine I built a small auxiliary brain, which controlled the lower part of Worf's body.

And finally, there was a scene in which the rehabilitated Worf must ultimately walk, but walk in bare feet. The producers wanted me to come up with a makeup device for Worf's feet that would make the Klingon anatomy even more interesting than it already was. So I constructed a series of spines that ran down the front of Worf's feet and built a makeup appliance that looked like a horn. For the fifteen seconds of footage that they shot of Worf's feet, the whole effect turned out very well.

The Klingon makeup continued to evolve throughout *The Next Generation* and on into *Deep Space Nine*, where Klingons became a presence on the space station.

DATA

The character of Data originated, according to Gene Roddenberry, way back in 1974 in Roddenberry's pilot for the series *The Questor Tapes*, about an android searching for a meaning to its own existence. Data was an android who had entered Starfleet and became an officer. Devoid of emotion, Data was seeking to understand humans and human emotions.

Part of the success of Data was his makeup. He looked human, but off-color enough and with strange-colored eyes that turned him into an alien even though he was supposed to have been a perfect specimen. The makeup staff came up with that look after days of painstaking experimentation with different skin colors—battleship gray, bubble gum pink, and yellow, and even unique hairstyles. For almost a week, everything the makeup did to create the look of Data didn't capture the essence of an android. Finally, they came upon the very pale gold look that came to define Data. His skin color, along with his yellow eyes and the artistry of Brent Spiner's portrayal, has brought Data to life.

Data's actual skin color starts with a beige base, called Shibui, into which two different colored powders—pale gold and bright gold—are mixed to create the glow. Then, once the powders are packed into the base, Data's hairline is penciled in and then his real hair is styled. Brent Spiner then puts in the yellow-tinted soft contact lenses that he wears throughout the entire day's shooting. This makeup hasn't changed measurably since the first year of shooting. What has changed are the types of electronics created for Data

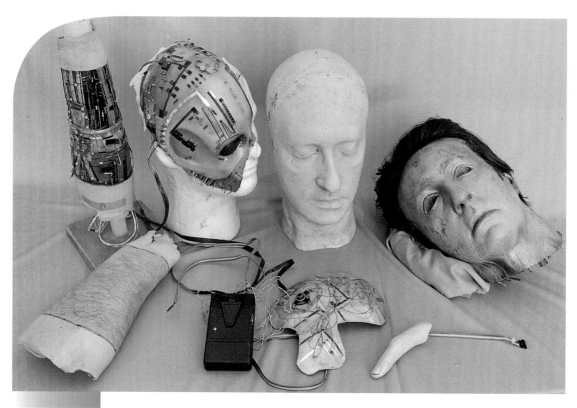

The many different
components
created to show
the android Data.

Robbie Robinson

as special effects and the different ways Data's limbs can be removed.

Creating the effects of Data's removable limbs, thereby enhancing the illusion that Data had been assembled out of parts, began in the first year of the show with the use of Brent Spiner's empty head mold as the form for a plastic head prop used in "Datalore," the episode in which Data discovers his brother, Lore, and learns the truth about his own past. Thereafter, Data's head as a prop was used on subsequent episodes, most notably "Time's Arrow." Data's removable arm was also used as a prop in "Measure of a Man," in which Riker is forced to prosecute Data.

The idea to add bits and pieces of electronics to Data actually started with the LEDs on the connecting points of Geordi La Forge's VISOR. And the inventor wasn't Michael Westmore, but his son, Mike, Jr.

MICHAEL WESTMORE

The idea for Geordi's LEDs came out of a conversation I had with my son as we walked across the Paramount lot to the production office. Michael, who had worked for me a few times in the past, thought we should have an interesting effect to indicate the contact point on the sides of Geordi's head when his VISOR was removed. So Mike, Jr. built a pair of little metal attachments that had flat bottoms and could be glued to LeVar Burton's makeup. They had wires running through LeVar's hair and down the back of his neck to a small battery pack underneath his arm.

It was these same blinking LEDs that we began using for Data to make some of the shots of his components more interesting. Probably the best example of how we developed these little groups of LEDs into a real circuit board was in the episode "Datalore" when the side of Data's head is exposed after he's kicked by Lore. In subsequent episodes, "QPid," "Disaster," and "Time's Arrow," we were able to create even more dramatic effects with rows of blinking lights. In "QPid," Data opens a flap in his arm to reveal a tremendous amount of light. This effect was possible because Mike, Jr., had built a new circuit board on material he'd discovered that was paper thin, so it could be wrapped around Brent's wrist, yet was resilient enough to hold a circuit that connected a configuration of LEDs.

In "Disaster," we combined Mike, Jr.,'s circuit-building expertise with an optical-illusion shot in which it looks as though Data's head has been removed and inserted into a special connection that links his brain to the ship's computer. The point of the sequence was to restart the ship's computer using Data's computer, which had just repaired its logic circuitry after having been nearly shut down by a computer virus that also shut down the ship's computer. But the visual effect couldn't look like Data's head was just pushed through a desk. So we staged the shot in which Brent had to remain completely still while he was underneath a platform with his neck wrapped inside a special collar that was really a basic circuit board holding a very elaborate array of LEDs. In postproduction, Brent's body was optically removed, and the result was an illusion in which Data's functioning head had been removed and hooked directly into the computer. It worked very well and even said something visually about Data's character that dialog alone couldn't have accomplished.

Perhaps one of the most complicated yet successful results we had with Data's makeup was for Lal, the young child android that Data builds in the episode "The Offspring." In the young android's first appearance, before the creature chose

Robbie Robinson

whether to become a male or female, we had to make it look almost sexless, so we built a square upper chest to cover the round shape of actor Leonard Crowfoot's pectoral muscles, which also camouflaged his nipples. Then we built an entirely new head appliance for him which fitted over his head, lowering his mouth line to where his real chin was. As a result, Leonard couldn't hear very well or breathe through his nose. We also had him wear silverized contact lenses, so he couldn't see very well either because of the diffusion of light. His breathing was so restricted that in between scenes, he had to hold his finger in the appliance's mouth hole in order to draw in enough air to keep him going.

To make matters even worse, Leonard was glued into a foam appliance that covered his crotch area and made it impossible for him to go to the bathroom, even in between scenes, or grab a bite of something to eat. Accordingly, he didn't eat the entire day during his shooting,

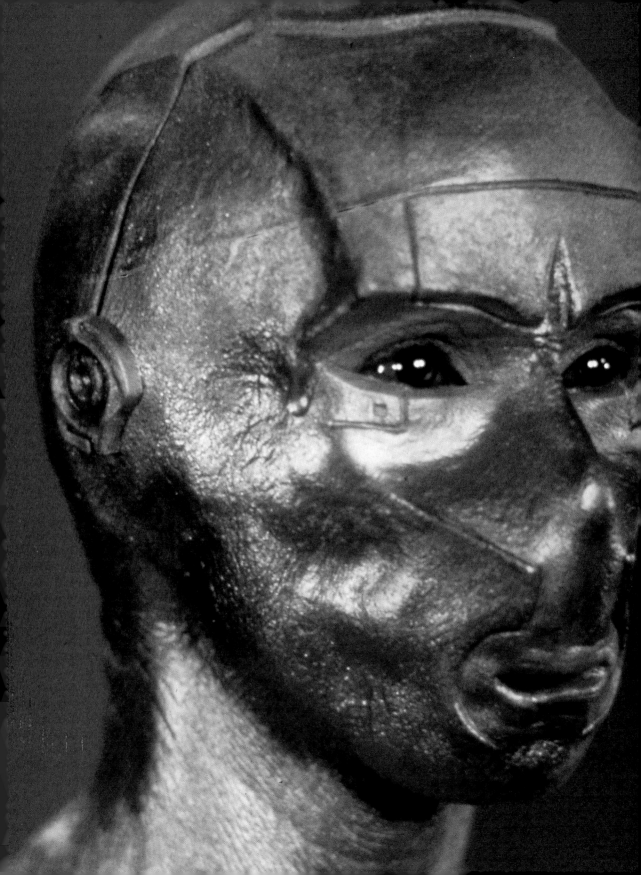

which turned out to be almost eighteen hours. He had a four-hour makeup session in the morning followed by twelve hours in front of the cameras and a two-hour makeup removal at the end of the day. Even the removal was tough, because we sealed him into his appliances using a makeup called Pax, which had to be scrubbed off with a loofa sponge. For three days, Leonard Crowfoot went through a grueling ordeal that was probably one of the most intense shoots that any young actor has had to endure. It was a credit not only to his professionalism but to his stamina and perseverance that he pulled off such a great performance while he could barely see or breathe and couldn't eat or go to the bathroom.

After Lal had chosen to become a young woman, actress Hallie Todd took over the role. Now it was up to Mike, Jr., to create an LED effect for a scene in the script that had to sell the entire idea of the complexity of the android that Data had built. In the scene, Data touches his "daughter," and the entire top of her head opens up. To create this effect, I built a fiberglass skull structure with a matching wig section. Mike, Jr. built an intense array of lights that drew a lot of power and couldn't stay on for very long because of the amount of heat the circuitry generated. So we knew we only had a few seconds to make this visual work.

For the shot, the camera was mounted a little higher than it normally was to highlight what was about to happen. Then, Data touches Lal's head, the appliance for which was attached to a piano wire and the other end of which I was holding off camera. On cue, I pull the piano wire to open the top of Lal's head, revealing a dazzling constellation of blinking lights. To the audience it looks as if Data has merely touched a switch that opens the android's head where her positronic brain is firing away. It was a

great scene that did the job of getting the audience to buy into the reality not only of Lal, but of Data as well.

Robbie Robinson

THE FERENGI

This race of "Yankee traders" evolved over the years from a hostile, opportunistic culture in their early depictions in *TNG* to a fully structured complex society as seen on *Deep Space Nine*. While in large measure the characterization of the Ferengi grew because of the writing and the performances of Armin Shimerman, Max Grodénchik, Aron Eisenberg, and Wallace Shawn, to mention a few, the characters were also effective because of a collaborative makeup design process.

The design concept began with color renderings of the aliens by Senior Illustrator Andy Probert. In the original concept, the Ferengi had large ears because they were especially attuned to hear sounds. The makeup department made some initial changes to the design, especially after the producers suggested that the large, sharply pointed Ferengi ears looked like oversized Vulcan ears and needed something to make them look more original. The producers also had a problem with the long chin of the design, making the characters, in their words, "look more like a witch than an alien."

The makeup department modified the design almost immediately to eliminate the long chin and round off the pointed ears. Then they added sets of wrinkles across the large bulbous noses to give them more character. The final makeup touch for each military Ferengi was a symbol, designed by Michael Okuda, that was hand-painted on the right side of the huge Ferengi cranial lobe and consisted of the symbol for the concept "dog eat dog" preceded by a rocker or chevron. No chevrons means that the Ferengi belongs to the lowest ranks, one to two rockers means that he's an officer, and three rockers stands for a command rank, almost a general. The symbols were painted green for the color of money.

After the episode "The Last Outpost," when the Ferengi next appeared in "The Battle," a set of lower teeth was added to the makeup, which made the Ferengi look even more carnivorous. In subsequent seasons, the makeup was enhanced to create cheekbones for the different characters that made them look more realistic. With the use of the airbrush technique in the later seasons, the Ferengi became more complex, adding shadows.

MICHAEL WESTMORE
I continued to play around with the design for the Ferengi teeth, one of my pastimes on *TNG* as the show progressed and I had more time to experiment with different ways of creating a better look for some of the alien characters. Ultimately, I decided to create unique sets of teeth for each of the actors. I began by taking a cast of the actor's mouth and then changing the upper teeth in the cast by covering

individual teeth with acrylic pointed teeth. I leave gaps between some or bring others closer together. Sometimes I even make double rows. Then I take a cast of the lower teeth and align the uppers and lowers to each other—sometimes even shooting a tooth into a gap between the uppers and lowers—so that when the actor speaks, his Ferengi teeth will open and close naturally.

One effect of the prosthetic teeth that I didn't figure on at first was that they made the actors all lisp to some degree or experience some other speech impediment. I like to give the actor his new teeth two days before shooting so he'll get used to them. He can then learn to say his lines and modify his speech to conform to the impediment. Often, I gave each new Ferengi actor a little speech welcoming him to a distinguished line of previous Ferengi and explaining what the teeth will do to his speech. It always worked, and the actor would bond to his teeth even more than the teeth bonded to him.

THE ROMULANS

Like the Vulcans and the Klingons who would return from the original series, the Romulans eventually came to play a part in *TNG* story lines. The challenge in bringing the Romulans back was to devise a makeup style that held true to the original concept that Romulans and Vulcans were related races yet differentiated them visually. *TNG* was a more complex show than the original series. Thus, Romulans—the warlike race that menaced Kirk and his crew—would have to be just as warlike and menacing but at the same time more complicated and as different from Vulcans as they could be without destroying the original concept of the two races. This was the visual challenge presented to the makeup department.

The challenge in bringing the Romulans back was to develop a makeup style that held true to the original concept that Romulans and Vulcans were related races yet differentiated them visually.

Romulans and Vulcans have the same skin color, the same severe hairstyle with different bangs, and the same pointed ears. The makeup department developed a new look for the Romulans, however, when they devised a special forehead appliance that had a dip in the center, bulged out over the slanted eyebrows, and was hollowed out in the temple area. It made the Romulan characters look as though they were always frowning while at the same time it wasn't so obtrusive that they looked like Neanderthals. The makeup department also gave itself the task of differentiating the forehead pieces so that no two Romulans looked alike. All in all there were ten or so different types of forehead designs for the Romulans so that each actor could be fitted with a separate design for any episode. There were even forehead pieces for Patrick Stewart and Brent Spiner when Picard and Data had to pose as Romulans in "Unification." A third variation was created for the proto-Vulcan look for the Mintakans. Jonathan Frakes and Marina Sirtis had to pose as Mintakans in "Who Watches the Watchers?" and wore additional forehead pieces as well.

The makeup department used the same base on both Romulans and Vulcans, which was called LN-1, the LN standing for Leonard Nimoy, whose character's makeup skin tone was the standard for the two races. It is simply a very light yellow base and then, depending upon the facial structure of the actor, the makeup artists apply different shades of green and yellow to create highlights and shadows. In this way, no two Romulan makeups in the same episode look exactly alike.

Romulan makeup takes about two hours to apply, with about 50 percent of the time involved with gluing the forehead piece and ears into place; the final hour is spent putting on the rest of the makeup, wigs, and eyebrows. The wigs are also interesting because instead of the flat look of Vulcans, the *TNG* makeup department

Michael Paris

added a short widow's peak to the front of the wig. The shape and depth of the widow's peak approximates the same basic V look of the forehead piece to reinforce the frown expression and make the facial expression look balanced. However, depending upon the hairstylist, the widow's peak can be so slight it almost looks like it's not even there.

Where necessary because of the episode and type of costume, the yellow skin tone may also be applied to the actor's neck and hands. For wounded Romulans with scars or bleeding wounds, the makeup artists use a green dye for their blood, in keeping with the color of Vulcan blood established in the original series.

MICHAEL WESTMORE

We tried to give the Romulan women a slightly different look from the men. Starting with Carolyn Seymour in "Contagion," I sculpted her forehead piece somewhat softer than the men's. She had the same frowning look but not the heavier boniness around the forward skull that the men had. Similarly, Denise Crosby's character, the Romulan Sela, was much softer than her male subordinates, not only because she was a woman but because her mother, Tasha Yar, was human and Sela was only half Romulan. We wanted to make her look more human than Romulan so we dispensed with the headpiece entirely and only gave her slightly pointed ears. Much of the Romulan look was carried by the skin tone and the wig.

With older Romulans, such as Tomalak, I added more wrinkles to the forehead and ears along with aging makeup to the rest of the face. That way, the appliances and makeup blend together to give an appearance of aging without turning the character into a cartoon. You have to make sure the appliance and the rest of the actor's appearance are seamless or

The makeup department used the same base on both Romulans and Vulcans, which was called LN-1, the LN standing for Leonard Nimoy, whose character's makeup skin tone was the standard for the two races.

else you will lose the magic of illusion.

THE VULCANS

Vulcans were the first alien race to appear on *Star Trek* and their makeup, even though it had evolved over the twenty-three years since the initial pilot, remained stable through the original series and the motion pictures. Although Vulcans appeared in the first season of *TNG*, it wasn't until the second season that Suzie Plakson first appeared as Vulcan medical officer Dr. Selar in "The Schizoid Man." For Suzie's Vulcan character, the makeup department started with the standard LN-1 makeup base, keeping the

Both photos:
Robbie Robinson

Vulcan skin the traditional light yellow color and adding the traditional hairstyle made famous in the original series.

At first, each actor playing a Vulcan on *TNG* had an ear appliance created especially for him. Eventually, the makeup department developed a number of standard sizes for different-sized ears. Ultimately, whenever a new actor came aboard to play a Vulcan, he was prefitted with one of the standard sizes that matched the configuration and outline of his ear.

Similarly, every pair of Vulcan eyebrows was also different. Some were dark and heavy while others were lighter. By playing with different combinations for Vulcans and Romulans, the makeup department was able to individualize looks so that the

combinations of forehead pieces, wigs, and ears all worked to reinforce the character in the week's script.

MICHAEL WESTMORE ON SAREK AND SPOCK

We had to establish the series on its own before venturing to bring back some of the Vulcan characters from the original series. Mark Lenard was the first, appearing again as Sarek and bridging the gap between the *Star Trek* motion pictures and the new television series. Because Vulcans have an extreme longevity, the years between Sarek's appearance in the motion picture and his first appearance on *TNG* didn't present us with any problems in designing his makeup. We decided not to age him, and the studio agreed, suggesting that we use the natural lines of his face as contours. However, for his reappearance in "Unification," we had to show the effects of the degenerative

Robbie Robinson

illness that had afflicted him. We again used the basic design and lines of Mark Lenard's face, but this time we aged him and showed him looking gaunt and drained. We used deeper shadows and placed rubber stretching around his eyes to show fatigue.

Leonard Nimoy's makeup for "Unif-ication" was treated much the same way as Mark Lenard was treated on his first appearance. Leonard came to the series straight from *Star Trek VI: The Undiscovered Country* and although eighty years had passed between the period depicted in the motion picture and *TNG*, the studio had advised us not to change Spock's makeup appreciably. Therefore, he looked basically the same as he did in the motion picture.

THE BAJORANS

The design for Bajoran makeup was essentially a design for the striking Michelle Forbes, who portrayed Ro Laren, the first Bajoran in the series. Michelle's makeup was very simple, because the producers didn't want to come up with anything that would detract from her looks. The makeup department started with a small bridge between her eyebrows and added a nose appliance with tiny ridges. Originally, there was a wing piece attached to the nose to make the character look more alien. However, because large numbers of Bajorans were also in the story, the makeup department couldn't handle that many individual winged pieces coming off the characters' noses, so many of the attachments were elimi-nated. Also, as more Bajorans were added to the cast in subsequent episodes, the nose pieces were modified so that some had five ridges, others four, while Michelle had seven. The Bajorans in the Cardassian

Michelle's makeup was very simple, because the producers didn't want to detract from her looks.

Michelle Forbes as Ensign Ro Laren.

Robbie Robinson

penal colony wore elaborate earrings, individualized for each actor.

THE CARDASSIANS

MICHAEL WESTMORE ON THE CARDASSIANS

The first Cardassian was Marc Alaimo, who later went on to play a Cardassian on *Deep Space Nine*. I already had a cast of Marc's head from "Lonely Among Us," a first-season role on *TNG* where he played the lead Antican, essentially a canine

character. Marc has an extremely long neck. I was asked to come up with a concept for the Cardassians at a time when nobody really had any ideas about what they should look like. I knew what Marc Alaimo looked like, and I already had a cast of him. The producers told me they didn't want a full head appliance for the Cardassian, but, following Gene's rules, the Cardassian had to be humanoid-looking and interact with the Starfleet personnel. I had to look for features that could define the Cardassian.

With Marc's long neck, it screamed at me to do something with it. That's where I began. I extended his look, which was a natural feature, almost into the look of a king cobra. This is how I combined an actor's appearance with my file of recognizable animal shapes. The point of recognition was a deadly snake, which, by the way, ultimately defined the essence of the menace of the Cardassians.

I started with the exoskeletal ridges of bone along the sides of the Cardassian neck, just like a snake, and connected them behind the ears. Then, to fill in the area between the ears and the jawline, we built up little bony ridges, did away with a human nose completely, and then I had the forehead left. What was I going to do with the forehead?

A year before I did the Cardassians, I was going to a Thai restaurant in Studio City. There was an art gallery next door and inside was a big picture hanging on the wall of a woman with a spoon in the middle of her forehead. I said to my wife, "I'm going to remember this. Someday I'm going to use this." And when I looked at the design for the Cardassians I was developing and saw that I had eliminated the creature's human nose and had this enormous space above its eyes, I thought of the spoon and put it right in the middle of the Cardassian forehead. Then I carried the ridges on the face around the eyes and up from bony ridges at the tops of the eyes to the top of the hairline and also around the sides of the face beneath the eyes. There are a lot of individual appliances for the forehead, neck, and head as well as special earlobes, underneath the nose, and across the chin.

The scaly ridges reinforced the shape of the eye and actually made the sockets bulge just a little to make the character intimidating. We gave them straight black hair tightly combed straight back so the hair created the same slick look as the rest of the body. Marc Alaimo, as Gul Macet in "The Wounded," was the only character to have facial hair, which looked out of place at first but set him off from the rest of the Cardassians under his command.

The design for the Cardassians worked as well as if not better than that for any other character on *TNG*. But the main feature of the character itself came from combining Marc Alaimo's own natural physical features. What we were able to do with the Cardassians is in contrast to what the creators of the original series were able to do with a character like the Gorn. Wah Chang had to work with traditional, hard rubber devices, a full rigid headpiece, and a full suit to get the look he wanted for the Gorn. The result was that as much as the Gorn moved, he still looked slow and cumbersome and almost ineffectual inside his headpiece and had none of the reptilian movements you'd normally associate with a deadly alligator.

Marc Alaimo as Gul Macet.
Robbie Robinson

Twenty-plus years later, the advances in makeup, foam latex appliances, medical adhesives, and sealants allowed us to re-create a reptilian look, but this time make the characters such a presence that the producers created an entirely new show centered on these characters and the Bajorans.

THE BORG

The original story concept for the Borg had described them as a race of insects. But even before the script was written, the original concept was changed to a race of cybernetic beings—human-machine hybrids who had an insectlike social culture, a hive mentality in which the drones relentlessly carried out the commands of the collective. The look and intensity of the Borg, the horror of their inexorability, and their adaptability to any sort of attack or defense against their weaponry made them formidable antagonists. They first appeared in "Q Who?" Much of the success of the Borg must be credited to the designers who first came up with the look of the characters.

The first concept for the Borg the makeup department saw came from costume designer Durinda Wood, who had sketched out a rough illustration showing a man in a suit with tubes running around it and plugged in at different spots. The sketches made it clear that the Borg look would have to be an integration of makeup and costume in a way that no other characters' had been before.

The original helmets for the first Borg in "Q Who?" were actually fabricated in the makeup department while the wardrobe people were assembling the suits out of a dark, almost black spandex-type fabric and metallic urethane. The two departments worked together initially to make sure that the helmet and suit designs integrated properly.

The helmet headpieces were made out of foam rubber cast from clay sculpture molds. Foam rubber was the material of choice so that the helmets would be comfortable for the actors to wear, especially on ten-plus-hour shooting days. The helmets were then colored to match the dark costume. An important element about the helmets was that they not be full head coverings. They had to look like alien headpieces hardwired into the brain, not bathing caps. That was why, even from the very beginning, the helmets only covered part of the skull, leaving other areas exposed.

When the helmets were completed and

The very first appearance of the Borg. Their look would evolve.

The look and intensity of the Borg, the horror of their inexorability, and their adaptability to any sort of attack or defense against their weaponry made them formidable antagonists.

in place, clamps were then attached to the headpiece for the Borg tubing that was already sewn into the suits to be run around the actor's body and attached to the helmet. With the helmet in place, the makeup artist attached the unique bits of machinery parts that help to individualize each drone. Originally, the parts were fabricated out of urethane, but eventually the makeup department started experimenting with other materials, such as old parts torn out of electric equipment and pieces of motors. These odds and ends parts actually looked high-tech, but in an almost hodgepodge way that reinforced the factory assembly-line look of the character as a recycled creature made up of whatever parts could be retrofitted. At the same time, it added to the distinctive look of each character so that no two Borg would look alike.

To make the character look even more machinelike, every time a costume left an exposed part of the body, such as half a head or an entire arm, the makeup artist ran one of the tubes directly into the exposed area. To make the tube insertion look realistic, the makeup artists created a latex appliance that looked like a bullet hole and glued the appliance directly onto the actor's skin. They then glued the tubes to the appliance. Where the actor's costume exposed a large area of bare skin such as an arm or shoulder, the makeup artist would run multiple tubes to make the character look as machinelike

as possible. The effect of having tubing running into the skin, especially into the actor's head, from the helmet and costume was so effective that the caps developed for the characters left more and more skin exposed so the makeup department could exploit the open areas with tubing and connections.

From the first appearance of the Borg, the makeup department realized that the actual color and tone of the creature's exposed skin had to underscore the element of the walking dead that defines the dronelike behavior of the Borg. Accordingly, the makeup base they chose was a product from William Tuttle's Custom Color Cosmetics in a shade called Shibui. The makeup designers wanted a dead-white look that blocked out all of the actor's skin tones. The Borg had to appear zombielike on camera so that the audience would know, viscerally as well as intellectually, that these were creatures devoid of individuality and reason and who would respond to their programming to such a degree that they would never deviate from their single function. The white makeup made them look lifeless, bloodless, as if individuality itself had been leached out. Before applying the base coat, the makeup artist glued the small foam latex plugs to the skin for the tube attachments. After the Shibui base coat was applied, the actor's face was then shaded to give him a skull-like appearance.

Ultimately, after encountering shading

problems in "The Best of Both Worlds" with some of the characters because of inconsistencies between makeup artists and their styles, the department decided to utilize airbrush techniques. Airbrushing was first used on *TNG* in "I, Borg" and quickly became a standard. This enabled the makeup artist not only to complete the Borg makeup faster, but to individualize the Borg so as to show that many different races had been assimilated.

Although the makeup department individualizes the Borg drones, the males and females are costumed to look almost identical. Where Borg drones are individualized is through the types of hand tools they use, such as cutters or plier-type devices at the ends of their arms, or through the types of electrical components or eyepieces they wear. In this way, the Borg are identified not by how they look but by the tools they wield.

MICHAEL WESTMORE ON THE BORG

Once the makeup base was applied and set with powder, I'd line up the actors like an assembly line and begin airbrushing them. I'd start with shadowing around the eyes. From there, I did the sides of the head where the helmet butted up against the face. Next I worked under the cheekbones and, finally, the backs of the hands. I liked the use of the airbrush because it gave me greater control over the final appearance of the character and was much faster for me to move down the assembly line than to give specific directions to individual artists. I used ComArt's transparent smoke gray because it gave me the shadows I wanted and still gave me the cadaverlike appearance of creatures who were, for all the world to see, lifeless but animated by an external force.

The Borg went through a number of modifications through the subsequent seasons, especially during "The Best of

Both Worlds." We not only had Borg mob scenes, but we had to Borg-ify Patrick Stewart with special electronics such as his laser headpiece. By the time we were creating Third of Five for "I, Borg," we were using airbrush techniques and even more elaborate eyepieces. The Borg were even more enhanced for *Star Trek: First Contact,* and then again in *Voyager* when the Borg became recurring characters.

Borg Electronics

Some of the most intriguing aspects of the Borg makeup consisted of the crystals, diodes, and accessories that adorned the Borg helmets and mechanical hands. There were miniature drills, buzz saws, calipers, lasers, and all sorts of gadgets that made it seem as if the Borg drones were put together out of a junk box in someone's garage. The truth is that's exactly how many of the eyepieces and accessories found their way into the episodes. The makeup department has taken castings from binoculars, pieces from model kits, odds and ends out of the studio trash, and even small crystal cubes that were fitted into the pieces. All of the eyepiece appliances are constructed out of foam latex. After they're painted black, the makeup artist burnishes them with a metal paste and they're ready to apply.

Borg Babies

In the nursery, incubated Borg start out as normal infants and then are gradually transformed by electronic implants. In the first episode where the Borg are introduced, "Q Who?," Riker, leading the away team, pulls out a drawer in the wall of the Borg cube only to find an infant. That infant was a real baby, the child of the executive producer's secretary. It was tricky to use a baby that small for the part, and it involved bringing the child in before shooting started so the makeup artist could take measurements of the child's head so that a dummy head approximately the same size could be found to create the mold. After the makeup department built a baby-size partial headpiece for the child, Mike Westmore, Jr., assembled a small electronics panel with blinking lights that was taped to the baby's chest and helmet.

As tricky as it was to fabricate the baby's Borg costume, shooting the scene was even more difficult. First of all, the cameras were only allowed to roll for a very short time because they could only get one take at a time. Also, the studio had to provide a nurse for the baby on the set. The scene itself required several takes, because each time the cameras started rolling, the baby would become fascinated by the black cord that ran from his head to his chest, grab it, and start playing with it. Although it was a funny scene and there were some people on the set who thought that a Borg baby chewing on his prosthetics might be a usable shot, Director Rob Bowman kept adding takes until he got a scene in which the baby left the cord alone. That was the take they used, and it wound up being one of the most effective scenes in the episode.

MICHAEL WESTMORE ON LOCUTUS OF BORG

One of the biggest challenges in "The Best of Both Worlds" was the transformation of Patrick Stewart into Locutus of Borg. In the script, we see that the Borg are actually operating on him, putting him through the transformation process from human being to Borg. So our challenge was to show how his humanity was gradually drained away in those scenes, building up the climax of the first half of the two-parter that spread over the third and fourth seasons of *TNG*. Rather than start putting him directly into Borg accessories, we started slowly by making his entire exposed body paler by a couple of shades,

showing that as humanity was drained away so was the color of life. When we see Picard at the end of the episode, he has already been transformed into Locutus and has become a complete member of the Borg collective.

For Patrick Stewart's full Borg transformation we wanted to leave enough of the Picard character visible so that the contrast would be startling. The audience had to know, through Riker's and Worf's eyes, that they were looking at the Captain Picard they knew, but that he was now Locutus. This was not only an important visual effect, but went right to the heart and soul of Riker's character, because Locutus had all of Picard's memories. For Riker to defeat the Borg, he had to defeat his own captain's abilities as they were wielded by Locutus. In other words, Riker had to fall back on his own unorthodox strategies to defeat an enemy commander who knew everything he did. Also, for Worf's startling line at the end of the episode introducing the final shot of Locutus— "He *is* a Borg!"—to have any real meaning, the audience had to see Locutus and Picard as almost one and the same.

We gave Patrick Stewart a full Borg makeup for the final scene in "The Best of Both Worlds, Part I": a partial headpiece that wrapped around the back, covered his right cheek, and came up under his right eye. Then we ran a tube through the headpiece to indicate that it was connected directly through his skull to his brain. There were also several tubes that ran through his suit into his body. On the side of Patrick's headpiece we mounted a small laser beam next to his right eye that turned out to be one of the most dramatic effects we were ever able to create.

The laser was the result of a conversation I'd had with my son about what we could do to make Patrick's Borg headpiece visually exciting. First we imagined what it would look like with a set of blinking

When Patrick turned his head to face the camera, he looked directly into the lens, and his red laser beam played directly into the camera. It made a great effect...

Patrick Stewart is transformed into a Borg.

Julie Dennis

lights. But then Mike, Jr., said, "Let's see what I can do with a mini laser if we can find one that will fit." So he researched it, called around to a few places, and found a device that was only an inch long. Then he built a holding chamber for it so we could find a way to isolate the beam of light it would throw off. Mike, Jr., threw on a tiny switch and we built the unit right into the side of Patrick's headpiece.

Now we faced the next hurdle: smoke. Since lasers don't throw off a visible beam you have to isolate the beam by firing it through a substance, usually smoke. Without smoke on the set it would be impossible for the camera to pick up the sweep of the beam, which was the effect we wanted to get for the cutaway for the season. Here is where Marvin Rush, our director of photography, came to the rescue. He found a way to fill the set with smoke. Now we could photograph the sweep of the laser.

The final challenge was to shoot the laser directly into the camera, which had never been done before so we didn't know how it would photograph. Just to play it safe, we told the camera operator not to look directly into the viewer when Patrick's laser was aimed into the camera lens. We rehearsed the shot without switching the laser on so we could choreograph the scene and plan for catching the great sweep of the laser as it came across the lens. Once we set the shot up, we just filmed it, hoping for the best and

crossing our fingers that the next day's dailies would show us we got what we wanted.

And the following day at the screening, we knew it had worked. When Patrick turned his head to face the camera, he looked directly into the lens, and his red laser beam played directly into the camera. It made a great effect, and in just a few weeks we knew that everyone watching the episode would stare directly into the laser and experience what we experienced when Picard announces that he is now Locutus of Borg and that any resistance is futile.

For the second part of the episode that led off the fourth season, we had to show how Patrick had been even more transformed by the Borg, because part of the tension would be how Crusher could de-Borgify him to return him to his human condition. And the audience had to be left wondering whether Picard could ever really be de-Borgified.

So this time we extended the headpiece to cover most of Patrick's face. We attached more tubes directly into his body and showed how his right hand had actually become a set of Borg tools. Then we also ran more tubes into the left side of Patrick's head and attached a sweeper mechanism to his eyepiece. This sweeper was also Mike, Jr.,'s invention, a device that connected to a servo motor and to a small battery power pack mounted on the back of Patrick's head. The wires ran from back to front but were mostly invisible to the camera because they ran through the rest of the gadgetry on his helmet. We placed a radio remote control unit off camera—the unit that flies model planes

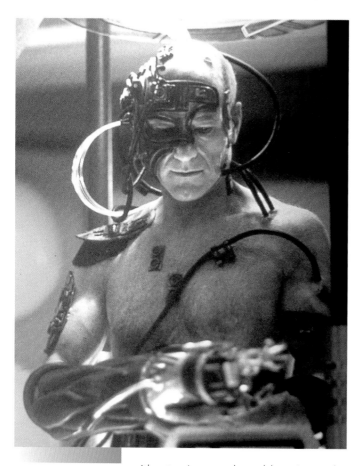

Showing the horrifying and dehumanizing process of assimilation, more appliances were placed on various parts of Stewart's body.
Julie Dennis

without wires—and could activate the sweeper motor with a flick of a switch. This was the Locutus that the away team snatched off the Borg cube and whom Data had to interface with in order to give the Borg the command to shut themselves down, thereby ending the Borg threat to the solar system and all of humanity.

THIRD OF FIVE AND THE EVOLUTION OF THE BORG

In the fifth season, the Borg returned,

this time in an engaging episode called "I, Borg," in which the *Enterprise* captures a young Borg barely alive after the crash of their scout vessel. The retrieval of the Borg gives the *Enterprise* crew an opportunity to plant a virus into Third of Five that might actually work its way through the Borg's neural network and destroy them. It was only Third of Five's or Hugh's "humanity" that halted this plan. The script, therefore, called for Third of Five to become a principal character, and that meant there would be a lot of close-ups on him. The makeup department looked for something special, something the audience hadn't seen before, to reinforce the importance of a lead Borg character.

The first effect makeup decided to create was a dramatic eyepiece that would capture the camera during close-ups. They'd already created a laser for Patrick Stewart, so this time it had to be something even more technically challenging. They came up with a hologram insert that changed shape when looked at from different angles. But the script also called for Third of Five, Hugh, to hand La Forge his eyepiece when Geordi asked for it. What could they create behind the eyepiece to show what a Borg's cybernetic eye looked like?

Mike Westmore, Jr., again designed an effect that made the scene work. When the original holographic eyepiece was fabricated, it was built with four magnets that clicked to the magnets on the helmet and held the device in place. The magnets on the helmet itself were constructed with holes in the middle. Mike, Jr., built a four-color LED array that sat behind the magnets on the helmet so that when Hugh pulled off his eyepiece and handed it to Geordi, the LED array, wired to a battery pack behind the actor's back, started blinking and set off a stunning effect that defined the Borg's electronic eye.

Third of Five's cybernetic tool arm was

also different from previous Borg arm and hand constructions. Instead of a heavy club arm, the kind of device that Patrick Stewart wore, the makeup department built a foam-rubber glove that covered his hand and forearm all the way up to his elbow and had plug-in attachments for all of the tools he would carry. One particular tool was a sharp point that could have been either a drill or a weapon and a plug that Third of Five used in a very effective scene to connect himself to the *Enterprise* power grid and reenergize himself.

MICHAEL WESTMORE ON AGING MAKEUP

The first time we used aging makeup for an actor was in the pilot episode,

The first character from the original series to appear in *TNG*, DeForest Kelley was "aged" for his guest shot.

when we aged DeForest Kelley, who played a very old Admiral McCoy. The production staff didn't want us to overdo Dr. McCoy, just a white wig and some wrinkles. I only added a small forehead piece to accentuate this one aspect of his look, and for the rest I stretched his skin and applied latex to create the wrinkles. Over the ensuing year and eventually over the entire seven seasons, we had the chance to create some incredible aging-makeup designs, beginning with "Too Short a Season," in which the episode began with an old Admiral Jameson, who then "youthens" because he's taking an antiaging drug. We started out with a complete bald head cap, a forehead appliance, separate pieces for the upper and lower part of the eye, a throat piece to accentuate the sagging skin, and jowls. The last item we added was a wig. This process was incredibly complex, because over the course of the script, at specific

stages, we had to remove individual items and replace them with others while we tightened up the wrinkles, added more hair, and ultimately brought him back to the young man actor Clayton Rohner actually was. The initial makeup process took over four hours to accomplish, and it was one of the toughest makeup jobs early in the first season of the show.

In contrast to Admiral Jameson, Diana Muldaur's aging makeup in "Unnatural Selection" in the second season was an easier process, because the actress already had a more mature face. The script called for a rapid change of appearance over the course of the episode when Dr. Pulaski is stricken with the Darwin hyperaging virus. As Dr. Pulaski's aging process accelerated after her encounter with the infected super-children at the Darwin Genetic Research Station, I was able to make intermediate changes to her appearance with creative shadowing and using stretch rubber here and there. For the final stage of Diana's makeup, we made a complete cast of her head and created a set of appliances that were appropriate.

Other than "Brothers" and the "Time's Arrow" two-parter where I had to create Mark Twain, most of the extreme aging makeup was applied to crew members in "Future Imperfect," Patrick Stewart in "The Defector," and to Patrick Stewart in "The Inner Light," which also required a gradual process starting with lengthening Patrick's hair—which always makes him look older—and ending with his final appearance as a very old man where none of his real skin was actually showing. In "Future Imperfect" the producers didn't want the principal actors aged too heavily, so we only moved them up by about sixteen years, with changes such as gray streaks for Marina Sirtis and Jonathan Frakes and a diabolical beard and mustache for Patrick Stewart.

The many faces of Captain Picard as realized by Michael Westmore and Patrick Stewart.
Robbie Robinson

Aging Patrick for his different roles, especially in "The Inner Light" and as one of Henry V's soldiers in "The Defector," was a particularly rewarding experience because of the way Patrick inhabited the roles. As understated as he was as Locutus, I think he was actually more powerful in "The Inner Light," because he had to portray a private individual, a family man over a number of generations, who was the complete opposite of a dominating authority figure leading his crew. Watching how Patrick accomplished what he had to do in this role, especially as he aged and had to face the destruction of his society, was very instructive because it not only showed how an actor can inhabit the make-up, it showed how he could animate it.

"Brothers" was a major feat for all of us

in makeup, but well worth the effort because of the performance Brent Spiner delivered not just as Lore but as Dr. Soong, the creator of Data and Lore, and also for the Emmy nomination we received that year. The first thing I did in creating the makeup for Dr. Soong was to build up Brent's cranial structure to suggest that he had more brain matter, literally pushing out the top of his head, than normal humans. We also had special contact lenses made for him to simulate the look of cataracts, covered his entire face with a thin layer of appliances, cast a new set of old teeth, and covered the backs of his hands with wrinkled skin as well. Shooting the episode was especially tricky, because the three characters, Data, Lore, and Dr. Soong, had to interact with each other.

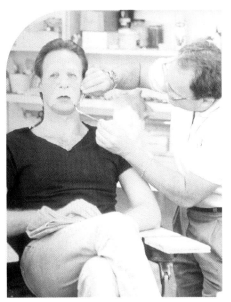
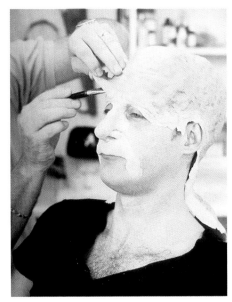

The writers had described Soong as "a ninety-year-old human...with more than a slight resemblance to Data."

Photos this page: Fred Sabine

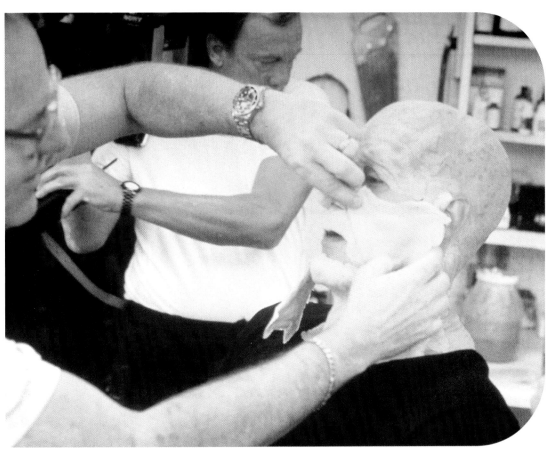

Below: In this take, Spiner has reassumed the role of Data and his stand-in is Soong.

Opposite: Brent Spiner as Noonien Soong.

Photos: Fred Sabine

"Brothers" was a major feat for all of us in makeup, but well worth the effort because of the performance Brent Spiner delivered... and also for the Emmy nomination we received that year.

This meant setting the same scene up at least three different times to get the principal actor in all three roles. In one particular scene where Dr. Soong reaches out to touch Data's face, we had to apply Dr. Soong's skin makeup to another actor's hand so that it could appear in the same frame with Brent's face and show an otherwise emotionless Data nonreaction to the gesture from his father. It was a very tricky scene, more so for Brent than

for me, but very rewarding when we saw how effective it was when the final editing was completed.

The two-part "Time's Arrow" was almost a marathon feat for everyone in makeup, not just because of our creation of Jerry Hardin's character of Samuel Clemens, which I created from a variety of photos of the writer, but because of the design of the Data heads, which were the landmark artifacts that led the *Enterprise* from

San Francisco to Devidia II and to the secret of the time-traveling aliens. To create the character of Mark Twain we built a nose, cheeks, and a chin. The rest

Jerry Hardin as Mark Twain.
Robbie Robinson

of the face was Jerry Hardin's with added wrinkles and a Mark Twain wig, mustache, and eyebrows.

ALAN SIMS ON *TNG* PROPS

One of the major similarities I shared as prop master on *TNG* with Matt Jefferies of the original series was that our requirements for the creation of the physical props of *Star Trek* sometimes overloaded the traditional manufacturing channels. Matt found that he had to go outside Desilu a lot, especially when it came to the fabrication of things like communicators,

tricorders, and phasers—the big three of *Star Trek* props for any shows—and went to Wah Ming Chang, who had been known in the industry at that time as a wizard, a magician when it came to assembling bizarre-looking futuristic props from things you'd find in any supermarket or hardware store. Wah told me himself how he looked for just the right screening material, simple industrial screening, for the microphone covering on the first handheld communicators for the original series. And he said that when you hold it in your hand and see what it's made of, you would hardly believe it would make the special effect you're after. But on film, when it's flipped open by Kirk or Spock, and married to the distinctive sound of a communicator, you believe it.

The story goes that Matt Jefferies was getting nowhere with the Desilu prop shop. So when he spoke to Wah and Wah actually brought in a mock-up communicator, Matt took it to Roddenberry and he was wowed. The idea of a flip communicator, which was nothing like anyone had ever seen in the early 1960s, was something that overwhelmed them.

When I first started on *TNG*, I would bring sketches of the props to the studio prop shop. At that time, some of the props that we had to have made weren't that critical. But as the first few weeks of the season progressed, I could see that some of the props would be extremely expensive to produce and time was crucial. I had to develop sources other than the prop shop.

The difference between *TNG* and other shows I'd worked was that when you do a police show or a period show, especially a Western or a detective show, the studio usually has a whole inventory of props you can use. It's relatively easy to assemble props for a Western, because they're already there and all you have to do is find them and modify something so that it

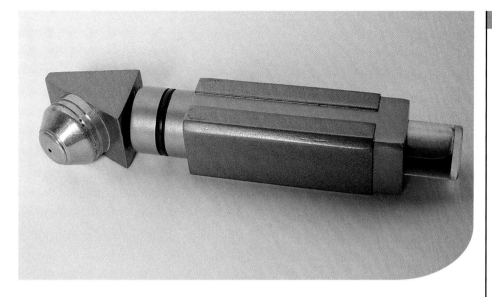

Robbie Robinson

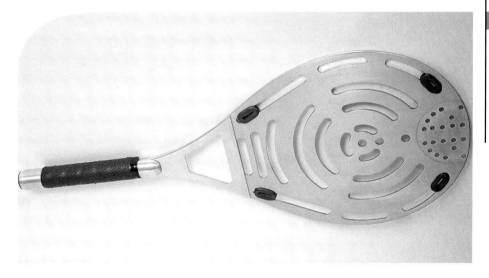

Originally created for Picard in "Suddenly Human," this prop reappeared on *Deep Space Nine* in "Rivals."

Robbie Robinson

fits the script requirements. *TNG* presented us with a quantum difference. Not only were the props not there—most of the material from the original series was long gone—but what you had to manufacture was wildly expensive and had to be of a certain quality to sell the effect. If something didn't look right, a phaser or medical device, the whole scene would collapse. Props had to hold up their end or the whole scene would look hokey. That was the first challenge I faced as a prop master on *TNG*.

The Combadge

The communicator badge was the easiest part of the job. It was already created by the time I came on to do the show and the whole device worked through an audio effect. Tap the badge and a sound effect is dropped in during postproduction just as with the flip communicator. Yet, it was all done with a simple stamped-out piece of metal and special effects. It didn't start out that way, however.

The earliest idea in *TNG* was to drop the wrist communicator, seen in several features, because it just didn't work for television. Then they said that they should hang a communicator right on the uniform just like the police wear today. But that turned out to be too big and not futuristic-looking. You could see police on the street with shoulder communicators so why would that remain the same for three centuries? They went round and round with the

communicator. Finally it was suggested, "What if the communicator was actually part of the uniform, a badge that identified you as Starfleet at the same time as it was a two-way device." It didn't have to open, you only had to tap it. So the combadge became the simplest prop of all.

The combadge is an example of what our job was as a production team selling a new show to an existing *Star Trek* audience. We basically had about two or three minutes for a new prop, if that, to make it believable. The tricorders and phasers were already part of *Star Trek* history and took very little to sell. Everyone watching *TNG* knew what a tricorder was, and whether it was a flip-top or a medical tricorder with a little probe, it had instant recognition. The phasers were also standard Starfleet equipment. But the combadge, that was another matter. The combadge had to sell an entire series, including a completely different cast in a brand-new version of the *Enterprise*.

Given that if a prop does or doesn't work, it happens immediately, the combadge, in particular, had about three seconds of screen life to see if it would carry because it was so simple. And it did. One tap and it was sold. Everybody on the show knew it worked because of the response we got. For the next seven years, the single chest tap became the signature motion of *TNG* the way the wrist flip became the signature motion of the original series. But this is how a prop works. You live or you die in a single scene.

The Small Hand Phaser: type-1 and type-2

The tiny hand phaser, or the type-1 phaser, had to make sense as a device that could project a beam. Until you had an infrared or similar remote control device that you aimed at a control panel on your TV, the motion of using a hand phaser made little sense.

One of the things we found about translating the look of props from the original series to TNG was that the device had to correspond to a reality that the audience could identify with.

When we first assembled for *TNG*, Gene Roddenberry didn't give us any specifics. He only said, "Give me drawings with a bigger or smaller but higher-tech look." The first *TNG* hand phaser, for example, looked like the handle of a Samurai warrior sword or a dustbuster. This look evolved through the first few seasons and then, gradually, we angled the handle, the design of which remained constant through the end of *TNG* and *DS9*.

The Tricorder

At the outset of *TNG*, Gene Roddenberry

After the first season the type-2 phaser—dubbed the "dustbuster"—was retired, this sleeker more militaristic phaser was created.

Robbie Robinson

announced that he wanted something smaller and cooler than the original tricorder. So we translated the flip of the original communicator to the flip of a tricorder device, replacing the handheld

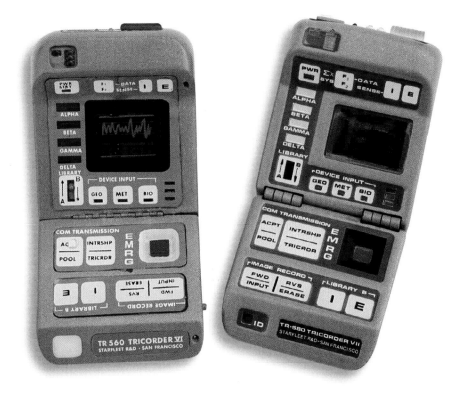

The tricorder evolved from the first-season Mark VI to the Mark VII.

Robbie Robinson

probe. We kept the original 35-millimeter screen that was a part of the tricorder from the original series, but hid it under the flip-up attachment. We could fit transparencies into the screen if the scene called for it. The medical tricorder was a little different in that we kept the flip-up component, but added the probe into a compartment on the top. The medical tricorder also forced the person performing the diagnosis to use both hands instead of just one. It made it look more medical, unlike the regular tricorder that away-team members used.

The communicator, tricorder, and new design of the phasers were all preconceived by the production staff well before I was there. Andy Probert's and Rick Sternbach's drawings made the props work, and then their sketches were translated into a physical reality.

Besides the tricorder, there were numerous electronic devices on *TNG* that originally came out of the Art Department and were then manufactured for us. As the series progressed, however, the incidental electronics became too expensive to develop this way, so I began visiting electronics stores to come up with casings and housings for things we could show on camera that looked more scientific than what we could design ourselves. Ultimately, a trip to Radio Shack or another type of electronics store was all we needed to come up with something for Dr. Crusher's sickbay or even one of the projects Wesley Crusher would experiment with.

Holsters

The phaser and tricorder initially went into cloth-sewn holsters or pockets that were Velcro-backed and fit onto opposing Velcro on the costume. We used these for about three years. But they became cumbersome because they interfered with the way the way the actors moved. You couldn't bend without difficulty or run without holding the tricorder or phaser pocket. As a result, we developed a rigid vacu-formed holster that we now attach on to the costume with World War II–era clips just as canteens were attached to the GIs' utility belts. So the twenty-fourth Starfleet uniform has as one of its main components a 1940s-style military clip that slides onto a sleeve sewn into the costume by the Wardrobe Department.

Backpacks and Utility Luggage

As futuristic as many of the props look, for things like backpacks and other types of carryalls, we found that we had to resort to twentieth-century design and shoulder straps to hold them in place. Sometimes it looks almost anachronistic to see Picard and Beverly Crusher rappelling down a mountainside wearing backpacks, but that's probably a technology they'll still use in the twenty-fourth century because it's utilitarian. You can fabricate the harness out of some space-age-looking material or provide it with a special ribbing, but it's still the same old harness.

Geordi's VISOR

Geordi La Forge's VISOR was another principal prop in the show that was essential to defining *TNG* visually. The VISOR was one of the central devices to the show because it was on camera with Geordi in every episode. The producers had created the character of the ship's control and flight officer who was blind, but they needed some sort of technological device to allow him to "see." They didn't know initially how the character was going overcome his blindness. Was it something worn on the forehead, a band, or something worn on the temples? The idea was to have something underneath whatever

he was wearing to act as a kind of sensor device, and these were LEDs designed by Mike Westmore, which came off whenever the VISOR was on. But as to the actual look of the apparatus, the producers weren't sure. That's when we came up with the look of the VISOR.

There were actually two VISORS, one for LeVar to wear and the other for LeVar to hold. The one he wore had an elastic band on it to hold it in place on his head and was combed under his hair. The one he carried had no elastic and was a bit wider than the one he wore. When LeVar carried the VISOR and you saw his LEDs, Mike Westmore would have to wire the LEDs with a a pair of leads that ran down LeVar's back to a battery pack. Then the LEDs would come off when LeVar's VISOR went back on. That's why there was always a cut between when Geordi reaches for his VISOR and when it's in his hand. It was to provide the place for a quick makeup change to get the LEDs in place and replace the VISOR.

After the second season, LeVar decided to get his hair cut shorter, and the result was that his hair would no longer hide the elastic band. So we had a real problem with the prop because the elastic would show. We redesigned the VISOR so that it had little tabs on the end that held Allen screws. When you torqued the Allen screws they held the VISOR to his temples through pressure. When the VISOR was in place, we'd slip metal disks over the screws so you couldn't see them on camera. And that's how the new VISOR was held in place, even though it would give LeVar headaches after a long day's shoot. LeVar truly hated wearing his VISOR and suggested many story lines that would allow him to get his sight back so he could get rid of his VISOR.

The VISOR was born out of a Michael Okuda design based on a hair clip. The device that Mike had worked up for

Our technology at the turn of the twenty-first century has already outstripped some of the technology from the original series.

Roddenberry had sensors running along the top of it and provided the basis for what would become Geordi La Forge's VISOR.

ALAN SIMS ON MATT JEFFERIES, TECHNOLOGY, AND PROPS

Matt Jefferies had a lot of questions for Roddenberry back in the 1960s about what the look of futuristic devices would be. He had to imagine how doors would open and what kinds of glasses people would use. Would people still eat with forks and spoons? Would we still have tables and chairs in the twenty-third century? Our technology at the turn of the twenty-first century has already outstripped some of the technology from the original series. So the questions Matt asked Roddenberry in his countless memos were valid.

I found myself asking Berman and Roddenberry himself many of the same questions Matt Jefferies must have asked. I'm still bothered by the fact that people may not eat with knives and forks three hundred years from now. Will they even eat at all or will they ingest nutrients from body packs when they're on board space vessels? But I don't want the audience to cope with these kinds of questions, because they have to relate to technology they know. The reality is we have to project today's habits onto events in the future.

As easy and elegant as the combadge was, the other props would prove to be far more challenging. After the first few episodes, I knew that the critical props for the upcoming shows weren't going to be up to the standards the show required. I found myself facing the same dilemma that Matt Jefferies faced: how to handle the material you're getting out of the studio shop, on deadline and under budget.

When we first introduced the Ferengi, in *TNG*, they used laser whips. The laser whip would function as a sharp coil when it was in its rest position. But in its attack mode, it would whip out and a beam of light would surround the whip section and create the illusion of a painful action. It was a variation of the *Star Wars* light saber. I had a thought that if we could only make this work as an automatic device that would coil and uncoil from a switch in the grip in some sort of vertebrae structure or rigid mechanism just by a flick of the hand, we'd have something. I realized that even if I had to have the Ferengi coil it by hand I wanted the whip to snap out automatically. That was the *sine qua non* of the prop: automatic snap.

I brought the Andy Probert sketches to the shop to have them manufacture the device. And with a seven-day lead time, we all thought this was feasible. As the week passed and I checked in with the shop, I was getting uneasy with the progress being made. Then, at the eleventh hour, the night before we were supposed to have this prop on camera, they called me and told me I'd have to take it somewhere else because they couldn't produce it.

I thought I would die. How could I take this outside in one night when the cameras roll tomorrow? So, now knowing that there would be no automatic function from the grip of the whip, I talked with the studio prop shop about making the whip end out of a band of flexible coiled spring steel that would automatically snap out to its full length when released. The characters would hold it coiled up and then release it so that it would snap out. Then we'd coat the spring steel with latex to make it sort of organic-looking. But, nonetheless, the effect of the prop had to be that it would snap out and look like an electronically controlled menacing device. However, when we used it for the first time, we let go of the coil and the steel sort of boinged out and shivered in the air. It looked kind of funny, actually, like a kid's toy. This made me very nervous.

Rick Berman saw me walking up to the set and saw me holding the whips. He stopped me and said, "How's our Ferengi whip?" I simply showed it to him and uncoiled it. You could tell he was disappointed. This wasn't the way I'd described it. I told him what problems I had with the manufacture and promised him I'd never let this happen again. He accepted that and with the use of smoke and other opticals on the set, you never saw the real failure of the whip to create the illusion. But I learned from that prop that I'd always give myself more time to scout around for just the right material and not rely on the promises of others that they could deliver. I would have to be the final arbiter of whatever prop was coming out of my office, because the shooting schedules and the demands of the show were just too stringent to allow for any slippage.

Therefore, for the ensuing years of *TNG* and *Voyager*, I built an outside staff of prop vendors who included Rick Gamez, John Fifer, Paul Elliot, and Al Apone from Makeup Effects Lab and Steve Hirsch and Mike Moore from HMS Creative Productions. Most of them are *Star Trek* fans and are very specialized. Some of them are electronics oriented,

others are fabrication and plastic oriented. I have a whole Rolodex of the kinds of people who can literally produce something for me overnight on the slimmest of descriptions.

As the show progressed, a level of trust developed between props and production to where we seldom needed sketches of the props anymore. In the beginning, we went through the standard operating procedure of sketch after sketch to develop the concept of a key prop. Then it was off to the vendor to fabricate the prop based on the sketch. But after a while, Rick and the producers would tell me not to worry about the sketches. Time was money, and the faster a prop could be created the better for everyone. So we eventually got to the point where they would look at me and ask if I understood what they needed for the prop and if I said yes, they simply told me to do it and not to worry about approval of sketches. That was how the

prop department and production eventually worked together after the first months of the first season. I really appreciated the way they let me invent the future.

In a script, for example, there might be a piece of stage description that says the alien is armed. I have to check with Mike Westmore as to whether the alien wears a prosthesis. What are the makeup and wardrobe considerations of an alien look, I have to ask, before I design the prop? That's how we coordinate before I build something with a trigger that the alien can't use because he has no hands. Similarly, I'll receive a sketch of a prop from the Art Department. Sometimes I've even asked for the sketch in advance because I need something to go on. Usually the sketch comes to me in black ink and I have to come up with a color scheme for the prop and that, too, requires my interfacing with Mike in makeup or with wardrobe to make sure that what I create integrates with what they're already working up for the character.

MY CONCEPT OF PROP DESIGN
Eating Utensils

This was one of the deceptively simple props that I had to develop for the show. We tend to take utensils for granted just as we take the very act of eating for granted. Yet when you look at the ways utensils have changed over the past four hundred years, you suddenly understand that you can't think of twenty-fourth-century eating utensils as something you order from the Pottery Barn catalog. They're not only different; what they look like conveys the atmosphere of the show. But you have to assume, for the sake of the show, that your viewers will believe people will still use utensils in the twenty-fourth century. So what I have to do is look for the unusual. Scandinavian and Danish are my favorites, because you rarely see them on people's tables and they look futuristic.

Card Games

The real anachronism that you see on *The Next Generation* are the card games. Riker's poker game with Data and his eye shade are some of the funniest sights in the series. Both the rectangular cards and the poker chips were throwbacks to the nineteenth century. But the producers wanted to keep some things unchanged for four hundred years, so the card games might well have been played in the Long Branch saloon in Dodge City circa 1885 or some Victorian parlor in San Francisco right before the 1906 earthquake. The only consideration for the future was that the poker chips were painted silver and brown instead of their standard red and blue.

Higher Resolution Television

Another big challenge for me and for Joe Longo, who was the alternate prop master on *TNG*, was the nature of television broadcasting itself. In 1987, sets were of a much higher and sharper resolution than the first color sets. The sets of the eighties were seventeen inches, twenty-one inches, or full wall-sized projection televisions that were much more demanding than sets of an earlier generation. We had to be more demanding about how the props looked.

We got away from the manufactured look, away from the plastics, the resins, and the bright paints. These don't translate on modern television sets. I went back to real materials such as metal, the stuff that phasers and tricorders would be made of in actuality. Obviously, they'd have different materials in the twenty-fourth century. Guns aren't plastic or resin, nor are high-tech medical devices.

When the actors handle the props, they feel the cold steel of a real object. They handle it differently, too. Also, the prop can't look like a one-off. A tricorder has to look as if it came off whatever assembly line Federation contractors use to provide

A first-season
chess set.

the devices to Starfleet. It's a further challenge, but a worthwhile one because a manufactured look imparts so much more reality to a scene. Therefore there's an entire machining process that goes into the preparation of a prop for a particular show. Anything less looks amateur.

The phaser rifles were another example of how the machined look worked for the show. Rick Sternbach created the look of the *TNG* phaser rifle. But where I contributed was in the manufacturing of the device. I wanted it to look like a standard military issue for the twenty-fourth century. The props had to *be* real. The phaser rifles *were* "real." They had the size and substance of a real metal alloy. They couldn't fire a phaser beam, obviously, but in all other respects they were manufactured as if they were real weapons.

Television is also your friend because the turnaround time between episodes might only be two weeks for a particular prop. If this were one of the *Star Trek*

features, you'd have months to do the same prop over again so it translates to a large screen. On television, you get very little time, but the time frame itself forces you to do it right the very first time. For example, we had to create transporter pattern enhancers for "Power Play." Colm Meaney, as Chief O'Brien, had to carry

The earliest version
of the type-3
phaser rifle.
Robbie Robinson

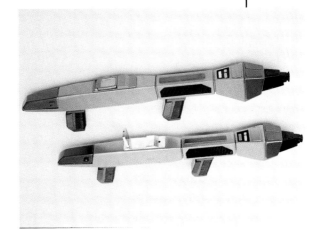

three of them to save an away team. I was afraid that the props, being made of metal, were too much for Colm to handle. But he was able to handle them, and the prop was reused by Joe Longo on *DS9* and again by me on *Voyager*. This is why taking the extra time to manufacture an item as if it were real instead of a prop benefits you not just because it enhances the look of an episode and an actor's performance, but because it lasts over time and becomes a permanent fixture.

Klingon Weapons

Here's another area where we didn't just create a single prop, we created a standard military look for the Klingon forces and treated each weapon from the disruptors to the *bat'leth* as if it were "real." The design and look of the Klingon weapons were the work of three men: Matt Jefferies, who designed the disruptors; Phil Norwood, who worked on *Star Trek III* and created the knife, the *d'k tahg*;

and Dan Curry, who worked primarily on *TNG* as a visual effects producer and created the *bat'leth* and many subsequent Klingon weapons.

In the case of the Klingons we developed a look of a weapon that would not just inflict injuries; they had to be weapons that would force you to get up close to your enemy. They were Asian-looking weapons, almost ninth-century in their design, that require you to use a kind of *tai chi* to wield them. They were weapons that spilled blood all over the place and forced the adversaries to wear

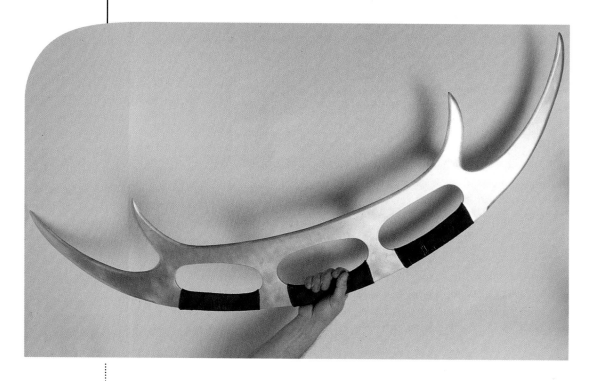

each other's blood. That's how the weapons worked to define the idea of a Klingon visually and to sell the idea of an alien race to the audience.

Borg Props

The very first Borg arms and hand tools on *TNG* were made by Rick Gamez and operated by me as a remote-controlled device off camera via a radio unit. We had little servo motors inside the arm that controlled the contraction of the pliers and the spinning wheels, and I ran these on cue from the director.

The Game

I built the mind-altering game device that Etana Jol uses to addict Riker and then the rest of the *Enterprise* crew out of a telephone headset. The device was physically constructed by the Makeup Effects Lab in North Hollywood after days and days of design consultation.

Back in 1987, simple phone headsets that freed you from having to stay close to the speakerphone on your desk were becoming very popular. Once we knew we needed the prop, the production staff and I spent a lot of time discussing how the device would look and work. It had to look as if it was almost magical in the way it stuck in your face and stayed in front of your eyes. Yet, it had to exist in the real world as a prop as well. I designed small strips of spring steel to form narrow, hollow fuselages that attached to the band of the headset that ran forward along the sides of the face to the cheekbones. Then I used small pieces of Lucite, heat-treated eliptical shapes that we bent back toward the actor's eyes and put little brass ends on them and held on to the steel fuselages by a ball and socket assembly. We put small coin batteries inside the side fuselages and LEDs that would light up when they were supposed to be on. All the rest was the actor's

imagination and optical effects to show what the character was supposed to be seeing through the eyepieces. The worst part about this device is that we had to build different units to fit on the different sizes of the actors' heads.

CHAPTER FOUR

The Next Generation

ALIEN ROLL CALL

THE TRAVELER

Portrayed by Eric Menyuk, the Traveler was a popular character, appearing in our very first season in "Where No One Has Gone Before." Eric's Traveler makeup consisted of a forehead piece that ran straight into his hairline down over the ridge of his nose, giving him a very pronounced cranial relief. He looked human, but very advanced. He also had a pair of oversized three-fingered hands that made him look alien and from a race whose hands had become very specialized, not needing the number of fingers humans need for manual dexterity. Because the makeup department had not begun to use the more advanced adhesives yet, the makeup for the Traveler wasn't very elaborate. When the Traveler came back to the show three years later, the makeup appliances were still the same. But we did change his skin tone to be more opalescent, and we redid his latex gloves to match.

Robbie Robinson

BYNARS

These very slight aliens appeared in "11001001" and were played by very young women who were not only exceptionally pretty, but exuded a childlike innocence. Like the Talosians from the original series pilot, these aliens were supposed to be unisex aliens. They communicated by looking directly at each other, at which point a flashing device on the sides of their heads would illuminate in rapid successive bursts, as if it were a very advanced electronic circuit emitting a signal. The devices were simple flashing lights wired to a battery pack mounted on the actresses' waists and controlled by the actresses themselves. It was very effective because it looked as though the creatures were actually having conversations with one another.

The makeup consisted of a large appliance for the head, fitted like a bathing cap, which came down across the bridge

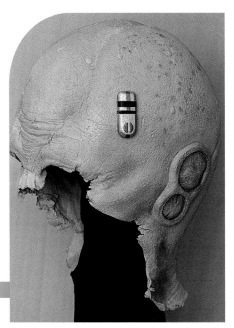

Robbie Robinson

BENZITES

The first Benzite character on *TNG* was Mordock, who competed against Wesley Crusher in the Starfleet Academy entrance exam for a single opening. In one of the most elaborate makeup designs for a first-season alien, the department had only a description in the script that referred to Mordock as wearing a vapor-breathing apparatus.

The makeup department created one major appliance that covered most of actor John Putch's head and additional pieces for his upper lip, chin, and eyelids. The eyelids John wore were an intriguing

of the nose, over the cheekbones, and around the neck. Because all the head appliances were cast from the same mold, each piece had to be modified, by cutting and trimming, to fit the individual actress. As a result the join line to the skin had to be covered up, and that was the reason for the purple hair on the sides of the aliens' necks. The aliens' ears were asymmetrical, as if each pair of Bynars formed its own unique symmetry, and the women were painted with a light purple shade.

configuration of puffy eyes with lids that folded back into themselves like Venetian blinds. Extending from the character's mouth area were a set of catfish feelers. Mordock's earlobes also had a set of short feelers extending from the tips. The Benzite headpiece was painted blue, but the makeup designer worked oranges and yellows into his skin color to make Mordock more lifelike.

Finally, because one scene called for Mordock to work on a computer, the makeup department designed a special

> **In one of the most elaborate makeup designs for a first-season alien, the department had only a description in the script that referred to Mordock as wearing a vapor-breathing apparatus.**

set of hands for the character that had two opposable thumbs, the "second" thumb slipped over the actor's pinkie.

••••

His mask was created with three holes for his mouth in case the makeup people on the set had to clean gunk out of the actor's mouth...

ARMUS

Armus was a creature who rose to his full and menacing height out of a black pool to attack and ultimately kill Tasha Yar. This meant that the stunt actor would have to be immersed in a pit of black goo—concocted out of a water-soluble methocel dyed with water-based black printer's ink to look like oil—and be rescued if for some reason he couldn't breathe. Therefore, his mask was created with three holes for his mouth in case the makeup people on the set had to clean gunk out of the actor's mouth if any of the openings became clogged. Plastic lenses were constructed and glued into the eye sockets so the gunk wouldn't get into the actor's eyes. The makeup department was inspired by the Creature from the Black Lagoon.

The creature's makeup consisted of a head and a bodysuit that was built for the episode by an outside company. But the suit had no provision for an airpack, so the actor had to hold his breath for the shot, which had to be timed with a stop-

watch, while he was lowered into the pit on a grate. Wardrobe fitted the actor's suit first and then makeup affixed the head—made out of a soft polyfoam with a latex skin over it—and walked him right to the grate, where he was lowered into the pool for the scene to begin.

Problems with the suit began almost immediately, because although the water-soluble slick was supposed to be inert, it reacted with the suit, which began to fall apart at the seams and disintegrated by the end of the first day's shooting. Makeup had ordered an additional suit as a backup, but by the end of the first day, asked the factory to prepare even more suits, four in all, all of which disintegrated after one day's shoot.

Robbie Robinson

PAKLEDS

The Pakleds were introduced in "Samaritan Snare" as a race of aliens who appeared to be slow-witted, off-putting, and harmless. They were supposedly so dim they weren't capable of creating their own technology. Accordingly, other races felt sorry for them. But beneath the innocent exterior, these were members of an extraordinarily sharp and downright nefarious race who would steal what was not given to them. The challenge to the makeup department was to come up with a design that conveyed both aspects of

the Pakleds without giving the story away. Casting hired a group of very portly actors whose naturally benign expressions even without makeup conveyed a sense of innocence. Then makeup designed whimsical faces consisting of appliances for their foreheads, cheeks, and a pointed lower lip. Specifically, makeup came up with a set of eyebrows that went up to the center of their foreheads, projecting a sense of underlying hopelessness about their situation. The department also designed a set of double-sized teeth. When the truth about the sneaky behavior of the Pakleds came out, the characters would be able to bare their teeth upon discovery.

so the makeup department could make a cast for his head as a mold for the elaborate makeup.

The Antedeans wore full overhead masks with separate pieces that covered the lower lip, the chin, and the front of the throat. Because the makeup department built the masks in two separate pieces, the actors were able to open and close their mouths, so the heads were actually movable. The actors also had a large fin made out of clear urethane that ran over the tops of their heads, further reinforcing the fish motif. The masks had extra-large eyes that could blink and sets of gills with giant air bladders that opened and closed as well because they were fed by

Both photos:
Robbie Robinson

The insides of the gills were painted shiny red so they'd look just like fish.

air hoses that were operated by stage crew off camera. The insides of the gills were painted a shiny red so they'd look just like fish. Unfortunately, nobody got to see the gills work because the show ran long and the scene in sickbay, when the Antedeans recover from their deep-space-travel self-induced comas, had to be shortened. In the scenes that never made it to the broadcast, the Antedeans open their eyes and their gills start flapping. The editor cut the scene right after their eyes opened, however, and nobody ever saw the gills work.

ZAKDORN

In "Peak Performance," the makeup department had to fit the makeup for the Zakdorns to the full, round facial features of guest star Roy Brocksmith. The department created a forehead piece, an appliance that went over his nose and upper lip, and two long pieces for each cheek that formed ridges that flowed back toward his ears.

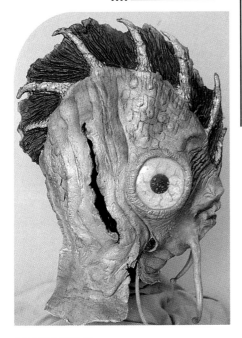

ANTEDEANS

The episode "Manhunt," with guest star rock musician Mick Fleetwood as a fishlike Antedean terrorist, was one of the more popular episodes in the second season of *TNG*. For Mick Fleetwood, the role of the nonhumanoid alien was so enticing that he even shaved off his trademark beard

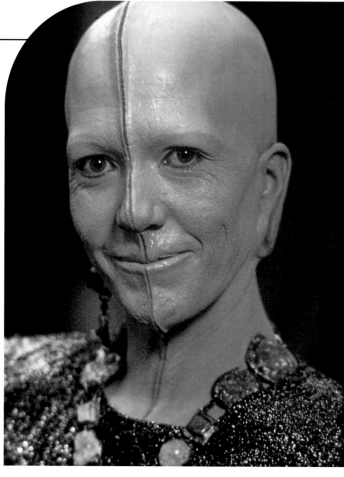

Robbie Robinson

**Roy Brocksmith
as Kolrami.**
Robbie Robinson

The basic design was used again for the Zakdorn quartermaster in "Unification," but refitted for a different actor.

LEYOR OF THE CALDONIANS

In "The Price," the hugely tall Caldonian Leyor was played by seven-foot-four actor Kevin Peter Hall. Working with an already interesting actor, the makeup department developed an elaborate forehead appliance for Hall which was oversized and extended and emphasized his overreaching height. His makeup was enhanced with the addition of a large headdress that wrapped around his forehead. Hall also wore special three-fingered gloves that changed the entire shape of his hands. Leading negotiations

for the Barzan wormhole was a Barzan whose makeup consisted of a much smaller forehead appliance with purple tubes that were glued to the sides of her face. Their makeup was an intriguing contrast to that of a Ferengi negotiator.

THE BOLIANS

The Bolians are one of the many races represented on the *Enterprise*. However, the first Bolian on the series was Captain Rixx in "Conspiracy," whose makeup was composed of a line of appliances that created a tiny ridge, raising his face to look as if it were split down the middle. The line ran from the back of his neck, over the top of his head, down through the middle of his face, over his nose and chin, down his neck, and under his collar. There were also extended earlobes and a dark blue watermelon pattern on the top of the head. Bolians are colored different shades of blue in order to portray a variety of skin tones.

ANTICANS AND SELAYS

The Anticans were furry-headed dog-like carnivorous creatures who applied for admission to the Federation. They were feuding with their sister planet, the Selay, snakelike creatures. The dog heads, essentially rubber casts, were created right on the lot at Paramount, but the Selay mask, made by an outside supplier, proved to be a problem. The Selay heads were supposed to be made of lightweight, four-pound polyurethane that would be flexible for actors to wear on the set the entire day. But the lab that fabricated the heads for the makeup department made them a lot heavier and far more rigid than anyone anticipated. As a result, the heads for the principal Selay actors had to be remanufactured at the very last minute with a soft foam rubber. Not that the dog heads were ideal; they only allowed for

minimal facial movement. To give the aliens some semblance of animation one scene called for one of the Anticans to stick his tongue out so that the character beneath the mask, at least, looked alive.

THE MALCORIANS

The Malcorians were another race, featured in the fourth-season episode "First Contact," whose minor physical differences from humans were important to the script because their culture had run parallel to Earth's in the twentieth century and because surgically altering Riker to pose as a Malcorian was one of the story elements. Therefore, there were very slight facial differences between Malcorians and humans, essentially a forehead appliance and webbed hands. The hands were interesting because in addition to the fingers that were webbed together, there were little suction grips at the fingertips and a suction cap on the thumb as well.

ULTRAVIOLET LIGHT BEINGS OF TARCHANNEN III

In "Identity Crisis," alien DNA, which had been implanted inside Geordi La Forge at the time he was a crew member on an away mission before he joined the *Enterprise*, begins transforming him into a reptilian being, invisible except under ultraviolet light. This was a gradual make-up, showing Geordi's mutation into a reptile until the final scene where he is completely changed and wants to remain on the planet. His makeup, a great collaboration between the wardrobe and make-up departments, consisted of latex bicycle pants, with hands and feet appliances, facial appliances, special contact lenses, and veins that six artists glued on by hand.

In the first stages of Geordi's transformation from human to ultraviolet reptile, little blue veins begin to appear on Geordi's

Robbie Robinson

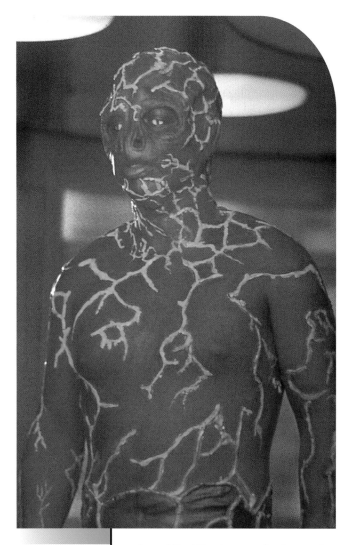

Robbie Robinson

**Right:
Franc Luz as Odan.**
Michael Paris

with a nose appliance that looked like a lizard's nose. The final transformation makeup took over six hours to apply, because it consisted of full appliances to LeVar's head, hands, and feet, and latex pants onto which the makeup artists glued each vein and then hand-painted them with a fluorescent pigment to make them glow under ultraviolet light. For a final touch, LeVar was fitted with special yellow contact lenses, prepared for him by Dr. Morton Greenspoon. The doctor's assistant then put drops in LeVar's eyes— the same ones that are used to test for glaucoma—that made the eyes glow when exposed to black light.

THE TRILL

neck, and like little streams of water coming together they start to connect. Each vein was a separate minuscule appliance that had to be glued on by hand. The more advanced the parasitic disease became, the more veins had to be glued on and connected. The same appliances had to be glued to Geordi's hands and feet at later points in the shooting of the episode to show the progress of the disease.

At the same time as the veins continued to proliferate, Geordi had to appear increasingly lizardlike, so at an intermediate stage of the transformation he was fitted

When Ambassador Odan became injured on a diplomatic mission, Dr. Crusher discovered that he was actually a member of a joined species, the Trill, who host symbionts implanted inside them. For the makeup department designing the first appearance of the Trill in "The Host," the challenge was threefold: the humanoid host, the abdominal cavity, and the symbiont. For this incarnation of the Trill, makeup devised an appliance for the nose and

116 | STAR TREK: ALIENS & ARTIFACTS

forehead to make them look just slightly alien but still overtly human. The real trick was the second requirement, the body cavity from which the symbiont would be removed and then inserted into Riker, the temporary host for the symbiont. Makeup created an appliance for the stomach area, covered with enough hair to blend into Franc Luz's own body, with three bladders underneath the false skin. In this way, the bladders could be activated, revealing the presence of the symbiont living inside Odan. Because the stomach appliance was created with very soft rubber, when air was blown through tubes into the bladders, the pulsating of the bladders was able to swell inside the entire area of the cavity, expanding it considerably, which made the shot very effective.

painted in a fluorescent paint so that it glowed when exposed to black light during the surgery scene.

THE J'NAII

The makeup department's design for the androgynous J'naii of "The Outcast" focused on blending over the differences between male and female facial features, such as eyes and eyebrows, as well as altering the female shape by taping down the actresses' breasts. The J'naii were played by women of different ages wearing light forehead pieces that covered their eyebrows. Each actress was painted with a very light flesh tone that made all of them look alike physically, but with enough difference in their facial expressions to allow for individuality.

The symbiont was a combination of a caterpillar's body attached to the head of an octopus with a few added convolutions to make it seem as if there were lots of brain matter.

Makeup also built a false torso for Jonathan Frakes for the surgery and the scene in which the creature is able to crawl into Riker's abdominal cavity. For the shot, the makeup designer, holding a line attached to the symbiont appliance, was lying under Crusher's surgery table. At the appropriate moment when the symbiont was placed on Riker's chest, the makeup designer pulled on the line to drag the appliance into the abdominal cavity. In the close-up shot, it looked as though the creature was actually burrowing its way into Riker.

The symbiont was a combination of a caterpillar's body attached to the head of an octopus with a few added convolutions to make it seem as if there was lots of brain matter. Inserted into the symbiont's head there was an air bladder that pulsated to make it seem alive. The head was also

KTARIANS

When Etana, a Ktarian, subverts Riker's mind, and the minds of most of the crew, with an insidious game device, the *Enterprise* finds itself in terrible danger. Part of Etana's ability to lure Riker depends on her dramatic beauty, a beauty that had to be represented visually despite Etana's alien physiology. Makeup was able to accomplish this by enhancing her female facial features. An appliance gave her a high, expanded forehead with bulbs for two large brain lobes. She wore a very beautiful red wig with full, rich hair. Her eyes were highlighted by powerful eyeliner and extra long and thick eyelashes, finishing out with seductive full lips. This was the first time we did a creative painting on fingernails. She was a very effective character.

Katherine Moffat
as Etana Jol.
Robbie Robinson

Opposite: Danny Feld

heads" by the staff, who wore large, yellowish heads with big nostrils. This show was interesting not only because of the ensemble aliens that were imprisoned, but because of the dual role played by Patrick Stewart, whose double on the *Enterprise* indulged in activities the real Picard would have shunned as captain.

BARCLAY'S PROTOMORPHOSIS SYNDROME

In an episode about paranoia and the realities that underlie our fears, Barclay (Dwight Schultz) receives a cure for flu that has ramifications for the entire crew. Everyone on board mutates into primitive life-forms. Barclay himself devolves into a spiderlike creature. Working with appliances and latex wrinkles on the top of Dwight Schultz's head and upper face, eye appliances, appliances that looked like spider's eyes, and a spider-leg device that protruded from the side of Barclay's head, the makeup department created a nightmarish vision.

VORGONS

In an episode called "Captain's Holiday," which featured the strikingly beautiful Jennifer Hetrick as Vash, Picard's love interest on an archeological dig for a deadly weapon, the Vorgons were visitors from the future sent to retrieve the device. Created from the look of a scallopy seashell, the Vorgons had crests that ran up their faces and all the way to the backs of their heads. There was one prepainted headpiece and additional appliances for the face and the throat. After all the appliances were attached, the makeup artists airbrushed color to match and then applied a coat of iridescent paint to create a glow on camera. Each Vorgon also wore an electronic earring that had a random pattern of blinking shapes and gave the effect that these creatures were indeed time-travelers from the twenty-seventh century.

THE "ALLEGIANCE" ALIENS

In "Allegiance," Picard's wits were tested against a race of aliens studying the reactions of their captives. A group of aliens were thrown together in a locked room. There was a Bolian woman, painted a lighter shade of blue than the Bolians' first appearance and wearing blue lipstick; a Mizarian who had a severely wrinkled and striated facial appliance with a hood over his head; a Chalnoth played by German actor Reiner Schone, who wore multiple appliances including a lion's mane wig, two sets of protruding tusks, heavy forehead vertebrae and sharply boned eyebrows with protruding horns or bone spurs, and red-and-yellow contact lenses to give his eyes an animalistic look; and a set of twins, nicknamed "cauliflower

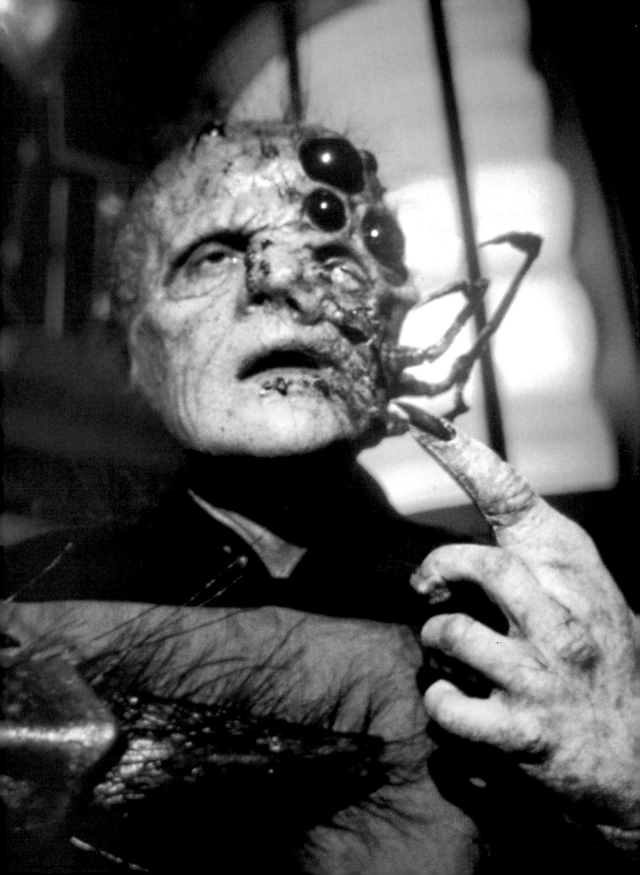

Robbie Robinson

THE ULLIANS

This race of telepaths differed from other aliens in *TNG* because instead of creating special forehead appliances, the makeup department designed appliances for the temporal areas of their heads using a pattern that looked like suction cups. The makeup artist applied the temporal pattern first and then laid hair over it to suggest that the design was a natural part of their skin, just the way wrinkles are on human beings.

THE SATARRANS

For a makeup device that was on camera for only a few seconds, this was one of the most elaborate creations ever to come out of the *TNG* Art Department. In the episode "Conundrum," the Satarran is a spy disguised as a human who, in the final seconds of the episode, is revealed to be a alien. The sequence in which the Satarran's human skin is melted away to expose his true appearance was done as a series of opticals, so the makeup department had to construct a head and

THE NAUSICAANS

In "Tapestry," the *TNG* version of *It's a Wonderful Life,* Picard's artificial heart fails after a fatal attack by terrorists during a diplomatic mission. Q gives Picard a chance to live by going back to the moment in time when his own heart had to be replaced. As a young ensign, Picard defends a fellow officer against attacks by ill-tempered but overpoweringly tall and ugly Nausicaans, who stab Picard, thus necessitating his getting an artificial heart. The Nausicaans made their appearance again in *DS9* as thugs and enforcers, owing in part to their effective appearance in "Tapestry" and their striking makeup, including hair styled in dreadlocks, braided along the side.

The facial mask featured a heavy forehead with a sharp line of bone down the middle and ridges extending to the side of the head, sharp bony ridges around the eyes, a flat snout, an oval for the mouth with two protruding intersecting tusks, and a split lantern jaw. Painted a near bone color, the face was in stark contrast to the thick hair and helped pull off their fearsome appearance.

chest, mount it on a platform, and then shoot it frame by frame. The opticals were added to the final shot.

TAMARIANS AND CAPTAIN DATHON

Paul Winfield's appearance as the Tamarian Captain Dathon was one of the highlights of the fifth season. An accomplished film and stage actor, Paul Winfield delivered a stunning performance.

Because Paul Winfield is a large man with a great presence, the makeup department realized that building alien features up through separate appliances would enlarge his head too much. So, instead, the department built a single piece that covered the actor's entire head and featured a bony ridge, almost like a central skull spine, over the top of the Tamarian's head down to his nose, which was more like a snout, and bony ridges on both sides of his skull. The three ridges looked like three parallel tracks of bone connected by a set of ridges that

Robbie Robinson

ran across the top of his head and down the bridge of his nose. His ears were large, but recessed, and there was a separate appliance for Paul Winfield's upper lip that was modified for the other actors portraying the Tamarians on their ship. The Tamarian coloring was added with hand-painted patterns of orange spots in patterns that were unique for each individual Tamarian, although they were all modeled on Paul Winfield's pattern.

Center photo:
Robbie Robinson

THE TAMARIAN MONSTER

The other principal player in this episode, albeit with an optical presence, was the gigantic creature that killed Captain Dathon and almost destroyed Picard. The makeup department built a huge head, first by creating a mold out of two hundred pounds of plaster and then by casting it out of polyurethane in three separate pieces. Also built by the makeup department was the creature's hands, while the costume department created the body. In the monster segments, the creature was assembled using computer-generated opticals that put the shots of the head, body, and hands together and enabled the creature to move and twist its head. For the closeups, the head was mounted on a stand and fitted with a lever that opened and closed its mouth.

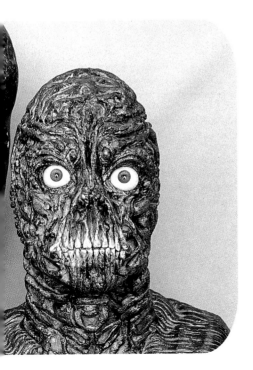

CHAPTER FIVE

Star Trek: Deep Space Nine

MIKE WESTMORE ON LIFE BESIDE A WORMHOLE

"More" was the word Rick Berman used to describe the types and numbers of aliens I'd be designing for Deep Space Nine. Here was a show that was as different from The Next Generation as any show could be and still be called Star Trek. On Deep Space Nine, most of the aliens didn't just appear for one episode and then vanish from the series until the producers decided to bring them back. A significant number of our aliens, we were told from the start, would be a constant presence, if not actually in the story, then in the background walking on the Promenade or in Quark's bar. The concept for the show was such that I knew we'd have so many recurring aliens that I'd have to plan way in advance by creating some standard appliance features that we could mix and match throughout the ensuing episodes.

Robbie Robinson

We knew that we'd bring back lots of the *TNG* characters such as the Ferengi, Bajorans, and Cardassians as well as the Klingons. I already had the essential makeup done for these basic aliens and, with the exception of a change in the makeup for the Trill, almost all of the major alien types were in the form they would be used. Odo would evolve over the course of the season, because I eventually went from several facial pieces to a complete mask, but his was a stable makeup.

The extra weeks gave me time to prepare a number of makeup heads for the aliens who would become part of the show. Not only could some of these heads be interchanged among actors playing aliens of the same species, these were heads that allowed the actors to talk, a major improvement from thirty years before, when the first heavy rubber original

series heads essentially immobilized the character and forced him to stand around as mute as a cigar-store figure. About 90 percent of the heads we created were capable of allowing the actors to speak. Even Morn could have spoken had the producers written that into the script.

After the show went into full production, the luxury of my doing sketches, working with the artistic designers of the show to come up with new alien creations, and other niceties that you normally have on a feature-film production schedule vanished. We quickly became overwhelmed by the pressure of scripts bearing down on us. At that point, for the first time, I realized that the nature of DS9, so different from TNG, forced the development of aliens whose presence might continue off and on through the series into a very tight seven-day schedule. I had to have actors' life masks sculpted and ready for design work as soon as the guest cast was

assembled. There was no time for tests. Whenever we completed the final face, we got right to work on it to get the alien look completed. Then the final clay design had to go off to Rick Berman for approval. From there, we created the appliances, full heads, or masks that the characters would wear, sculpted and poured and ready to wear in less than a week, sometimes, but usually in six days.

Where I wanted a background head to fit more than one actor, we didn't bother with final sketches because I didn't know who was going to play the part. When you know the guest star, you can make some sketches based on the actor's look, especially if the makeup will leave lots of the actor's face visible. This was especially the case with actresses such as Nana Visitor and Terry Farrell, whose extraordinary looks are what makes the characters come alive. But if it's just an alien who has yet to be cast, you have to go with your interpretation of the character described in the script and believe that your instincts are your best guide. Usually they are.

What enabled the makeup department to keep churning out the alien appliances each week was our ability to modify our backlog of appliances, the tons of molds from TNG that I'd prepared, and by saving the new molds from each episode of DS9, within a short period of time, I'd stored enough molds to modify or to copy for any new actors hired to play a guest "alien." And if we came up with something really neat, we could always use it again for a background alien walking around the station to fill up space on the Promenade or at Quark's tongo table.

Part of what I learned from DS9, even more than from TNG, was that the sheer pressure of the workload forced us not only to keep whatever worked as a piece for another alien, but not to abandon something just because it didn't work the first time. Even though we didn't have

Robbie Robinson

time to test—maybe especially because we didn't have the time—I refused to give myself the luxury of discarding something that didn't work for a particular actor or a particular alien. If I built it, I'd find a way to reuse it, I told myself and the rest of our department. And maybe that's why the *DS9* team worked so smoothly and had a number of appliances and makeup pieces to recombine when new aliens came along at the last minute.

We ran rubber all day long, gallons and gallons of it, and used up hundreds of pounds of plaster every week. Each day I'd get in at six in the morning and we would run rubber appliances and fabricate plaster casts of the heads we were building.

Some of our best discoveries came

Top:
The unique look of Altovar (Victor Rivers) was just one facet of the makeup that won the team an Emmy.
Robbie Robinson

Bottom: With 1960s hair and makeup the regular cast was able to "blend in."
Robbie Robinson

from mixing ideas to come up with a neat-looking bladder that we could tuck inside a temple or forehead appliance, or an eyelid that opened in a curious way. These became the basis for entirely new makeup designs and allowed me to create a look for *Deep Space Nine* that made the show stand out and will endure in reruns for years to come.

Perhaps one of the most enjoyable makeup challenges we faced was in the shooting of "Trials and Tribble-ations," when I had to come up with makeup that matched the colors of the 1960s. Since I was working in television in the 1960s, I knew the colors and the makeup Fred Phillips and the original *Star Trek* team had used. These were colors that had to

Right:
Nana Vistor as
Major Kira Nerys.

translate into black-and-white because there were more black-and-white sets in use than color ones. Many of those same makeups and colors were still available in the 1990s, and the hairstyling department was also able to match the styles of the 1960s. But redesigning a show to blend in with thirty-year-old clips was challenging.

KLINGONS

Worf was brought to *DS9* as a regular character, which enriched the show because of Michael Dorn's ability to energize the role, and he became a catalyst for the other actors. His presence affects every scene, not just because of the by then iconic Klingon makeup, but because of the audience's expectations whenever Michael was on camera.

It isn't surprising that Worf's makeup didn't chang a bit from the third season of *TNG*, with the exception of his hairstyle. Forehead vertebrae, skin tone, and all other aspects of his makeup were finalized during *TNG* and have remained the same. The original concept for Worf, all the way back in the first season of *TNG*, was Gene Roddenberry's insistence that he have a military haircut in keeping with Starfleet regulations. In the second season, the producers wanted to try the hair a little longer. They started by letting the hair out in a new wig they had made and

In "Blood Oath,"
Michael Ansara
recreated Kang,
his "favorite" role.
Robbie Robinson

...he became a catalyst for the other actors. His presence affects every scene.

THE BAJORANS

Michelle Forbes as Ro Laren was the prototype Bajoran that the makeup department began working with for *Deep Space Nine*. However, when Nana Visitor was offered the part of Major Kira Nerys, the makeup department made a number of subtle modifications to her look. First, they enlarged the nose ridges and made them farther apart. More important, they removed the wing from the tips of top of the nose because they gave the department a problem with the frown lines across people's foreheads.

"When I saw myself in the Worf makeup my first thought was, 'My career is over.' But Worf was written as a gruff and surly character, and the makeup made me gruff and surly, so it was easy getting into character.

"While the make-up was being applied I read the LA Times and I did the crossword. That way I couldn't see what they were doing to me.

"Michael Westmore's a god. Seriously, Mike makes the alien come to life, day in and day out, and for that you need a lot of imagination and patience. And he has both."
—Michael Dorn

not trimming it as short. Then, little by little, makeup experimented by curling the wigs and then allowing the hairstyle to become longer and longer to give the impression that Worf's hair was growing. In reality, the hairdresser simply wasn't curling the wig as tight as it might have been.

Michael Dorn himself finally suggested that the best look for him would be for Worf's hair to be allowed to remain long, but to be pulled tightly back into a pony-tail. He pointed out that with his hair left long and uncontrolled, it would fall into his face every time he had an action scene. His hair had gotten to shoulder length and was soon falling over his shoulder, swinging around every time he tried to move. Pulling it back, he said, would keep it out of the way. It also brought Worf back to a military look and was simply a more convenient style for him to wear. Once it was changed to a ponytail, it was left that way through the rest of *TNG* and into *DS9*.

Many of the Klingon characters from *TNG* appeared in *DS9*, carrying over the theme of the rebellion of the Duras family. A new addition, however, was General Martok, whose scarred face and alley-cat missing-eye look brought a new dimension to the old Klingon warrior concept. The makeup department talked about a Martok with his eye restored, but everyone, from the producers to the actor, liked the one-eyed Martok so much, he remained the same through the final episode.

FERENGI

All through the appearances of the Ferengi on *TNG*, the makeup department had a one-head-fits-all policy. When Armin Shimerman was cast as Quark, that policy changed. The original heads were relegated to Max Grodénchik, Aron Eisenberg (Rom and Nog) and to the background Ferengi. A newer, larger head was constructed, something that would be more comfortable for Armin to wear. And to make the head appliance more comfortable for him, makeup sculpted holes in the sides of appliance for Armin's ears to go through so they wouldn't have to be flattened. His ears fit inside the ear appliances. The "new head" allowed Armin to stand out.

Eventually two customized heads were developed, one for another Ferengi, Jeffrey Combs, called Brunt, and the female Ferengi, whose ears were smaller than the males'. For the grand nagus, the makeup department started with the basic Quark head appliance and made larger ears and a more wrinkled forehead and neck. Thus the Zek head contains additional pieces that are glued on over the top of Quark's head so that the grand nagus looks older and far more wizened than either Quark or his brother Rom.

Below: Armin Shimerman is transformed by makeup artist Karen Westerfield.

"In the first year, the sight in the mirror of a nearly completed Quark would inspire me to become the character. In the second season, I began to take great fascination in the changing morning light as it played out on a cement wall, the way the wall color would change as the sun came up. I couldn't help feeling that I was trapped in Plato's cave with its meaningful shadows. What I learned when I wore special makeup was that there was a fine line that needed to be walked. Michael Westmore had given me this wonderfully 'alien' face that immediately signaled the viewer that I was otherworldly."

—Armin Shimerman

All photos: Robbie Robinson

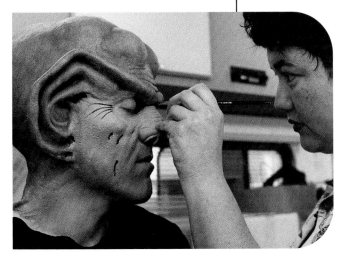

"There is no question that Michael is a *genius*. I never failed to see him in the wee small hours of the morning making sure his creative dreams were literally being fleshed out. The genius part comes in when you realize that the aliens always rang true. There's yet another *unsung* contribution by Michael Westmore. His enormous kindness and the reassuring manner that he has with actors who sit there while he applies the needed prosthetics, tattoos, plaster, or hairpieces. I have seen many skittish celebrities quieted by his humanity and reassurance."
—Armin Shimerman

Clockwise
from top left:
Hêlen Udy as Pel.

Jeffrey Combs
as Brunt.

Wallace Shawn
as the Grand
Nagus Zek.

Cecily Adams
as Ishka.

All photos:
Robbie Robinson

Another Ferengi development concerned the way the makeup department enhanced their teeth. The original *TNG* Ferengi had sharp jutting upper teeth but straight lowers. In *DS9* the makeup department added a set of lower teeth to fill the gaps in the uppers and give them an even more piranhalike appearance.

The designers made molds for the lower teeth to fit into the spaces between the upper teeth so the characters could talk, even though it affected their speech. The Ferengi also had blue painted fingernails, and Zek was given longer false nails.

CARDASSIANS

The Cardassian makeup is essentially the original makeup that Marc Alaimo wore in *TNG*, with the exception of the facial hair, which was removed. The make-up department added new molds and resculpted the shoulders, earpieces, and noses, making them more in keeping with the serpentine look of the species, but nothing basic was changed between *TNG* and *DS9*.

Clockwise from top:
Marc Alaimo as Gul Dukat.

Mary Crosby as Natima Lang.

Makeup extends quite a ways under the actor's costume to ensure that no "humanity" shows up on camera.

All photos: Robbie Robinson

MICHAEL WESTMORE ON THE TRILL AND THEIR SPOTS

Once the change was made from the *TNG* Trill to a Trill with spots that Terry Farrell played, I painted them by hand for each and every episode. For the five hundred and thirty-eight times I applied the Trill makeup directly onto Terry's skin, no two times were ever the same. Even though I conformed to the Trill spot pattern that hung in her trailer, the placement of the spots was always different each time she was made up.

At first, we made Terry up to look like the no-spot Trill character from *TNG*, with the forehead appliance. Rick Berman saw it and immediately wanted it changed. He wanted Terry's extreme good looks to be emphasized, not impinged upon by the makeup. That's why he wanted a new design. Rick kept modifying the original

"Why don't we try to do something very different with Terry and give her the spots we had on Famke?"

TNG design to the point where there was nothing left for them to modify. Finally, Rick remembered the very intriguing *TNG* episode "The Perfect Mate," with Famke Janssen as Kamala, a mesomorph who had spots running down the sides of her face. Famke was also one of the very early considerations for the Jadzia Dax role. Rick suggested, "Why don't we try to do something very different with Terry and give her the spots we had on Famke?" It was up to me to figure out a way to do the spots so that they'd show but not get in the way of Terry's looks.

I experimented with running them down the sides of Terry's neck. I used a number 3 watercolor brush to paint different kinds of spots, different colors, different shapes from round to elliptical. I started off at

Top to bottom:
Nicole deBoer wore Dax's spots for the final season.
Robbie Robinson

Hanging on a trailer wall was this pattern, the only *guide* used for applying Dax's spots.
Michael Westmore

Famke Janssen as Kamala.
Robbie Robinson

first with aqua color, but that could be sweated off under the hot production lights on the set. I tried marking pen but that still would rub off. Then, I went to a tattoo color that is water impervious and takes alcohol to remove it; it could still rub off under her collar. That's what I used. And I could spot her in twenty minutes, ten minutes a side. I could have used an airbrush, but that could smear. Also the airbrush is too precise. I wanted to soften the edges with a hand paint brush. I did two colors; the basic color was brown, but I highlighted it with a burnt orange. So it was a two-tone spot that gave it more reality and looked like it was part of her rather than a tattoo.

For those episodes when Terry's character was either very scantily clad or supposedly naked, I had to put spots in places where people would see them, such as down her leg or under her armpits. Then I had to use a larger marking pen. That took about an hour or two to complete.

ODO AND OTHER SHAPE-SHIFTERS

The makeup department learned most of what it needed to know about Odo from the character's description, which said "Odo was a creature, a shape-shifter, who could change into anything he wanted to, but could not realize a human face of his own. He could not do the fine details of his own face." So the department began by taking a cast of Rene Auberjonois's face and then started off by building his makeup up with small pieces. But, inside of the first few episodes, they realized that it just wouldn't work. Odo was too complicated a makeup to build up with

> Odo was a creature, a shape-shifter, could change into anything he wanted to, but could not realize a human face of his own.

A running gag on *DS9* is finally answered: "How far down do those spots go?"
Robbie Robinson

Opposite:
Terry Farrell as
Jadzia Dax.

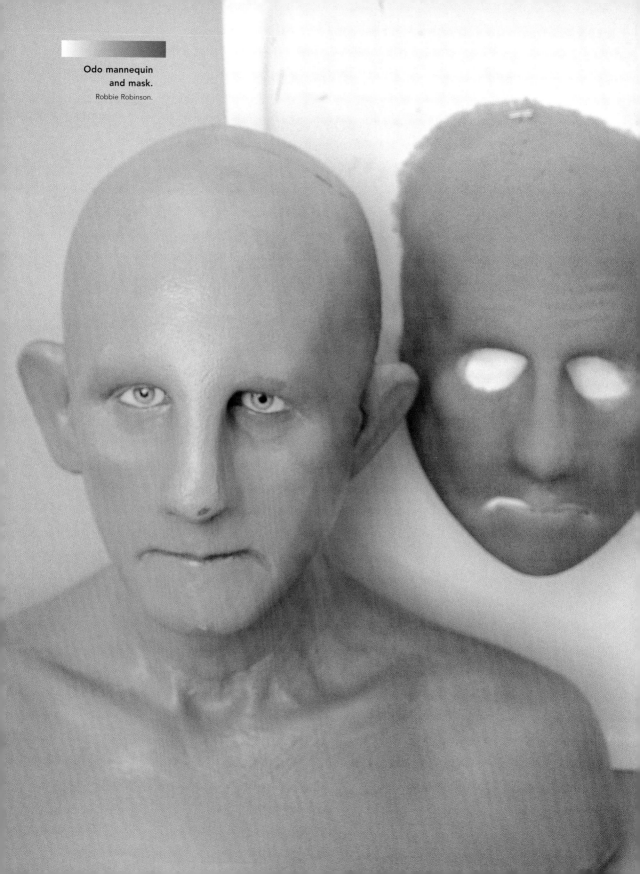

Odo mannequin and mask.

Robbie Robinson.

individual parts because the actor's skin texture wasn't at all like the smooth texture the character description called for. So the department built a single full mask for Odo and that became the basic look of Odo for the rest of the episodes.

The department tried to use the Odo mask for other changelings as they began appearing in later episodes, but some of the faces of the guest stars were so unique and different that Rene's mask could not be a one-size-fits-all appliance. Ultimately, the makeup department had to build new masks for principal changelings.

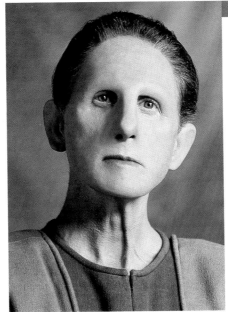

"The mask that was the main 'feature' of Odo influenced the voice and the physical/psychological gestures of the character. To this day, I find it difficult to project the voice of Odo without the mask."

"It is impossible to overemphasize the importance of Michael Westmore's contribution to the success of *Star Trek*. I never tire of admiring the creativity and seemingly endless imagination of Michael's work."
—Rene Auberjonois
Julie Dennis

Left:
Rene explains, "I try not to eat anything that might damage the makeup. I usually settle for some yogurt or soup, which I carefully spoon past my 'outer layer.' Once when I was called into makeup for touchups after lunch, I sauntered up to my lovely leading lady and engaged in what I thought was some clever banter. It was met with a rather strained reaction. As I settled into my makeup chair I glanced in the mirror and to my horror, there was a long stream of pea-green goo dribbling down my latex chin."

Robbie Robinson

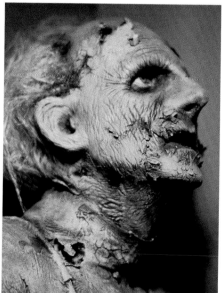

Top right:
A new face was sculpted, incorporating deep cracks in it. On top of that mask, little flakes of latex were glued to make it appear as if they were hanging off Odo's face. Sheets of the color latex were also glued to Odo's uniform.

Robbie Robinson

When Odo became Curzon in "Facets," some of the features of the actor who had played Curzon were incorporated into Odo's mask and Trill spots were added.

Robbie Robinson

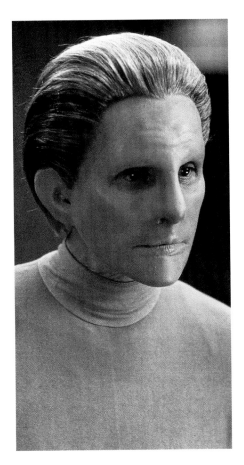

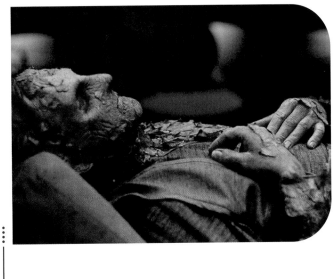

...more than just another fearsome alien.

THE JEM'HADAR

The concept of the Jem'Hadar was that the producers wanted something more than just another fearsome alien. They already had enough of those. For a group as powerful as the Founders, the producers conceived of a completely genetically manufactured race, the perfect soldier bred for the task with a need to follow and obey orders. Controlled only by a genetic addiction to a substance known as ketracel-white, the Jem'Hadar killed without it.

The makeup department searched for a look that depicted toughness and resiliency. The design they came up with was inspired by the rhinoceros, the toughest-looking animal in the jungle. The top of the head was based on a type of dinosaur like the triceratops, bony and reinforced with hard plates. The rolls that run down the neck and the scaly structure of the body, however, are a combination between a rhinoceros and a dinosaur. The rhinoceros design was carried over the top of the Jem'Hadar's face plates with a hornlike hairstyle down the back of its head and neck.

The first appearance of the Jem'Hadar.
Robbie Robinson

The first concepts for the Jem'Hadar were also built on the premise that these creatures were all clones and, therefore, looked identical. However, as they became more deeply woven into the story lines they almost took on the role of principal actors and had to be individualized. That presented makeup with the challenge of coming up with distinct looks for the different Jem'Hadar warriors. Makeup began by changing noses on the characters so they could be distinguished in a scene. Then, by the final two seasons, when the war between the Dominion and the Federation reached its greatest intensity, Executive Producer Ira Steven Behr wanted even more changes to the look of the Jem'Hadar; this would allow them to have critical roles in the final season's stories. So makeup added new bony plates to different Jem'Hadar as well as horn implants with different configurations to make them look more ominous and dangerous. Finally, special effects provided another Jem'Hadar look by coming up with a way the ketracel-white could be shown flowing into an individual warrior.

As the seasons progressed, more features were added to the mask, making the characters more identifiable. The mask created for Ixtana'Rax (Fritz Sperberg) clearly set him apart from the "Alpha" Jem'Hadar. Robbie Robinson

Jem'Hadar. "Don't spend a lot of time with a new face," the producers told makeup. "Just do something with the ears." Accordingly, a set of large, extended ears that didn't look too bizarre were designed, and combined with a pale skin tone to create an ominous and menacing look. Then, as a finishing touch, makeup came up with the idea of purple contact lenses for their eyes, highlighted by a lavender eye shadowing. The hairstylist worked up a hairstyle to go with the pale, slightly purple tinge. Female Vorta had smaller ear appliances to differentiate them from their male counterparts.

Molly Hagen as Eris. This was the first appearance of the Vorta.
Robbie Robinson

Jeffrey Combs as the Vorta, Weyoun.
Robbie Robinson

THE VORTA

The Vorta were a species that had to be created very quickly to fill a specific need: the Founders' managers, a bureaucracy that facilitated the will of the Founders. At the same time, the producers had made it clear that they didn't want an elaborate alien makeup, just an instantly recognizable humanoid creature who would interact with the Federation personnel as well as with the Founders/changelings and the

"Don't spend a lot of time with a new face. Just do something with the ears."

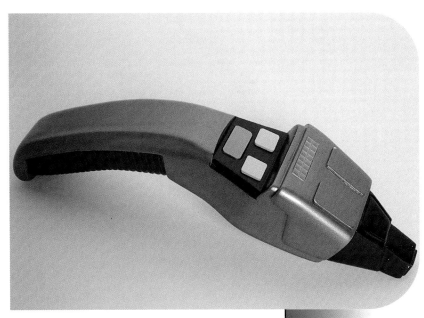

ALAN SIMS ON
DEEP SPACE NINE PROPS

The creation of the universe of props for *Deep Space Nine* was the brainchild of Property Master Joe Longo as well as Art Department personnel such as Rick Delgado, Rick Sternbach, Jim Martin, and John Eaves, who were responsible for the concepts underlying not only the phasers and tricorders, but the whole range of tools and accessories and, of course, the wide range of Cardassian field control units and phasers that were introduced in the show. In many ways, the manufacture of *DS9* props was very much like the manufacture of *TNG* props. Joe Longo's job was to find ways to get these concepts turned into reality, and HMS and Proper Effects were the places where these items could be turned out in a timely fashion.

As DS9 neared full production, we still had the time to utilize the same manufacturing techniques we did on TNG which was to find outside sources that could make the weapons, tools, and medical

equipment look as if they were constructed on the assembly line even though, in the *Star Trek* reality, many of the devices were replicated. We wanted to show that they were still industrial-grade weaponry and devices and not one-offs. This approach to construction of the props also extended to the various hand-to-hand weapons of the Klingons and, now, the Bajorans.

Beyond the official weapons paraphernalia of the Federation, the Bajorans, the Klingons, and the Cardassians were the items that filled out the look of the show. These were items such as the religious articles of Bajor, the Orbs and the trappings

Clockwise from top left: Like any good organization, Starfleet R&D keeps improving the tricorder. Here's the Mark X.

The type-2 phaser was redesigned to hug the actor's form.

Dan Curry created this Klingon weapon, a mek'leth, at the request of Michael Dorn.

All photos: Robbie Robinson

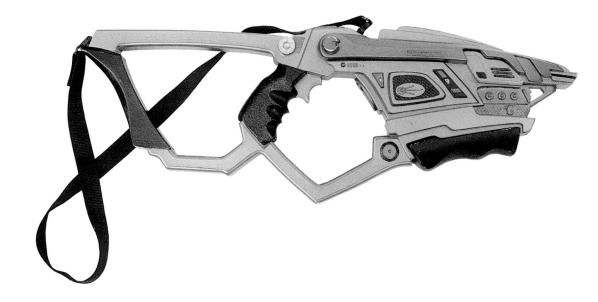

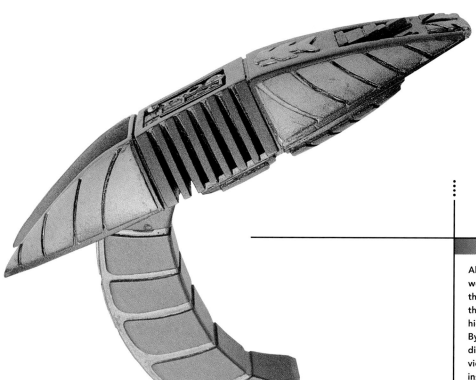

All new weapons were designed for the two races that would be highlighted on *DS9*. By creating very distinctive forms, viewers could tell instantly which was the Bajoran (top) and which was the Cardassian (bottom) weapon.

Robbie Robinson

Adding to the verisimilitude, padds were created for all the major races that would work on *DS9*: (clockwise) Ferengi, Cardassian, Klingon, and Bajoran.

Robbie Robinson

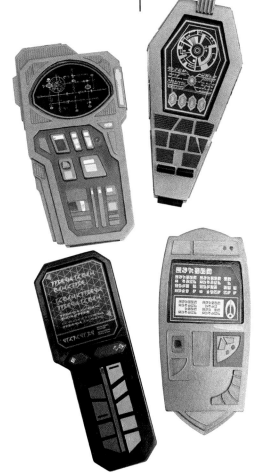

Knowing that Bajoran religion would play a large part in the series, great care was taken in creating this Bajoran Orb case. First seen in the pilot, this prop would be used over the entire run of the series.

Robbie Robinson

The sculptor of this prop used photos of Quark as reference, unaware that it was destined to be the staff of the grand nagus.

Robbie Robinson

Demonstrating true star power, a tribble—really no more than a stuffed round ball of fur—manages, once again, to steal the show.
Robbie Robinson

Joe found a battery-powered toy spider at a local garage sale, worked with an electric motor repairman to speed up the motor, and then had the device made up in Mike Westmore's shop.

of the Emissary, as well as Ferengi articles and Zek's official standard of office, the walking stick of the grand nagus.

Then there were the incidental items, props that came out of the producers' needs based on a specific script, such as the re-creation of a 1947 military base for "Little Green Men" when Quark, Rom, and Nog find themselves time-warped back to Roswell, New Mexico. Property Master Joe Longo also had to build his own tribbles for one of the most interesting episodes on *DS9*, "Trials and Tribble-ations."

Joe's other famous prop was the *palukoo*, a Bajoran spider, a handmade device based on a Jim Martin sketch. Joe found a battery-powered toy spider at a local garage sale, worked with an electric motor repairman to speed up the motor,

and then had the device made up in Mike Westmore's shop. Mike added latex features, eyes, and fur, and affixed a spike spine, and Joe had his spider.

The other demand on the *DS9* property department was the background props that were all over the station. You see them everywhere, but most noticeably in Quark's. Here, the property department was required not only to come up with a variety of food props, but with the odds-and-ends bottles and glasses that Quark would use in every episode. What we found was that you couldn't build these. Not in your wildest imagination could you come up with designs more fanciful and evocative than the manufacturers and distillers themselves who had to sell their brands on the same liquor store shelves with scores of other expensively designed bottles and decanters. So the best place to find the bottles and glasses for Quark's was in a bar or package store where the work had already been done for us. By discovering the special-edition bottles used for Jim Beam or other popular brands or by finding bottles at garage sales or swap meets, with the addition of labels created by the art department we were able to fill the shelves at Quark's not only imaginatively, but realistically.

A *palukoo*, native to the moons of Bajor and tag sales.
Robbie Robinson

An amusing label on this bottle of scotch demonstrates the fact that the Art Department knew it would not appear on camera.
Robbie Robinson

On the left, hung with a lovely gift tag, is a bottle of *kanar*. A Cardassian drink, the serpentine shape evokes the reptilian race. First seen on the original series, Saurian brandy could also be obtained at Quark's.
Robbie Robinson

CHAPTER SIX

Deep Space Nine
ALIEN ROLL CALL

MICHAEL WESTMORE ON *DEEP SPACE NINE* **ALIENS**
The mix-and-match aliens that dominated the Promenade of Deep Space Nine *as well as Quark's bar came to be known as "Westmore aliens." Production would call me up and say they needed a Westmore alien, which meant they would send the actor over in costume and I would work from my existing stock of appliances and heads to fit a look to the costume. I would begin with a previous head (sometimes, after the launch of* Voyager, *even a Neelix head) and take appliances from existing DS9 or TNG aliens such as noses or cheeks, or perhaps different faces made for principal aliens along the way, and add an adornment such as a Cardassian appliance. Then I'd paint them different colors or add spots so as to disguise them, and that's how I'd come up with a new alien for walking along the Promenade or sitting in the bar.*

MORN

Starfleet officer.
Robbie Robinson

When *Deep Space Nine* started, the producers told the makeup department to come up with ten new characters with no specific design that could be used along the Promenade or in Quark's bar. On the first day of shooting, when the ten characters paraded across the Promenade, the director saw the alien that would become Morn and said he wanted him to be a bar character. He told him to sit on a stool at the end of the bar, and that's where the character remained for the next seven years, with the exception of "Who Mourns for Morn," when he faked his own death.

TOSK

This Emmy-winning makeup was based on the scales and coloring of an alligator.

Above, left: Dabo
girl and Quark.

Above, right:
Scott MacDonald
as Tosk.

Right:
Mark Shepherd
as Morn.

All photos this page
Robbie Robinson

The back of the head was a dark greenish color with large, thick scales, while Tosk's face was like the belly of an alligator in a lighter yellow-green with smaller scales. Then the actor playing Tosk, Scott MacDonald, was fitted with special "slit" contact lenses for a reptilian look and was fitted with tiny fanged teeth and special hands. Because the Tosk costume had such a deeply cut neckline, part of the makeup included a layer of scales for the actor's upper chest.

KOBLIAD

Actor Caitlin Brown played Kobliad security officer Ty Kajada, rescued from her destroyed vessel and brought to Deep Space 9. The producers wanted just a minor set of appliances. Makeup created a ridged forehead that ran from her pulled-back hairline down to the tip of her nose and a forehead piece with an extended set of ridges.

WADI

For the Wadi the makeup department used different combinations of colored paint on the forehead. The designs were cut into stencils and airbrushed onto the forehead.

**Joel Brooks
as Falow.**

Peter Crombie
as Fallit Kot.
Danny Feld

Daphne Ashbrook
as Melora Pazlar.
Robbie Robinson

Randy Ogelsby as
a Miradorn.
Robbie Robinson

THE MIRADORN

This alien makeup design consisted of a forehead piece and a throat appliance with two bands of vertical latex down the front of the throat.

FALLIT KOT

This design consisted of a full face with a flesh connection between the nose and the chin so that when the character spoke, the bridge of connecting flesh over the front of his mouth actually vibrated. The makeup department was able to create a durable and realistic rubber ridge that looked and moved like a piece of flesh in one of the more unique designs for a *DS9* alien.

ELAYSIANS

Melora Pazlar was an Elaysian whose light-gravity planet made it difficult for her to move about DS9. A love interest for Dr. Bashir, Melora was originally conceived of as the science officer for the space station. Because she was involved in a romantic relationship that had to be believable for Bashir, the producers wanted her to have a strange-looking forehead but wanted no extensive makeup below her eyes. So the makeup department designed an enhanced forehead device that ran from the ridge of her nose and stopped there. She also had a blond wig with a receded hairline to allow for the forehead appliance.

THE SKRREEA

These were characters for which the producers wanted no appliances at all.

Instead, they asked that the makeup department create a skin texture that made them stand out. The makeup designer suspended tiny clay balls into a layer of latex and applied that to the surface of the actors' faces. When it dried, the coating looked like a layer of skin with hundreds of bumps spread throughout. Although the first test subject looked like a human with a terrible skin disease, the entire group of actors together looked like a race. This became a very interesting look, especially when topped off with a hairstyle that raised the characters' hair high off their heads, but kept it well groomed at the same time.

TORA ZIYAL

This character, the daughter of Gul Dukat and a Bajoran woman, had deemphasized Cardassian features. Since she was half Bajoran, she had a skin tone lighter than a Cardassian and a Bajoran nose.

HALANANS

Played by Salli Richardson, the Halalan Nidell Seyetik was the wife of Professor Gideon Seyetik. At the same time she was

Above, left: Deborah May as Haneek.
Robbie Robinson

Above, right: Melanie Smith as Tora Ziyal.
Danny Feld

Robbie Robinson

also the psycho-projection Fenna, who was engaged in a romance with Ben Sisko. The producers wanted nothing to detract from the actress's natural beauty, so the makeup department designed a pair of double-tipped ears that were never used again.

CHAPTER SEVEN

Star Trek: Voyager

Running two weekly series at the same time is always a challenging job for makeup departments, especially when the same personnel design the look of the aliens for both series. This job was even tougher for the Voyager makeup department, because the entire premise of the show was that the Starship Voyager had been catapulted into the Delta Quadrant of the galaxy, where nothing was the same. There were new life-forms, new dimensions where aliens lived, and plenty of Borg, because they inhabited this quadrant.

"Chakotay's tattoo design is a compilation of several native cultures. The makeup was tested as a full facial tattoo, but Rick wisely decided not to detract from Bob Beltran's looks. The design is hand-painted each day. A number three watercolor brush is used with blue tattoo ink. By the end of *Voyager*, it will have been re-created 750 times."—Michael Westmore

Opposite: Robert Beltran as Chakotay.

SIDE-BURN BIBLE
STAR TREK

A. CREPE-WOOL MUST MATCH NATURAL HAIR COLOR
   (BLENDED HAIR IS better Than a single COLOR)

B. LAY WOOL IN DIRECTION OF NATURAL GROWTH

C. ONLY TOUCH ENDS OF HAIR INTO THE glue

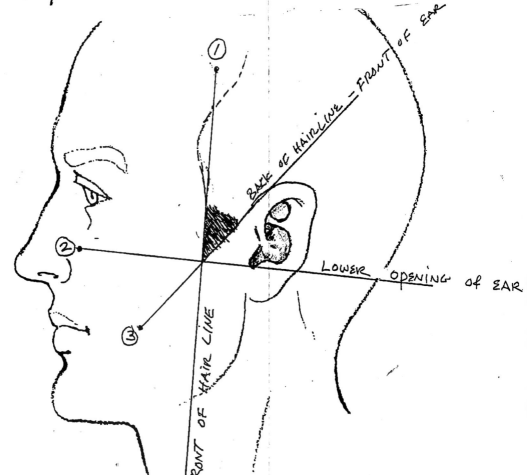

VULCAN

For Tim Russ as Tuvok, the makeup department used the standard Vulcan makeup from *TNG*, including specially sculpted ears.

TORRES

Torres was a half-Klingon made up to be lighter-skinned than a full Klingon but darker than a human being. Her forehead vertebrae were also smaller and she did not have Klingon teeth.

THE OCAMPAN

The concept behind the character of Kes was to hire a very pretty young actress who had a pixie quality to her and to reinforce that quality through the makeup. Most pixies or Peter Pan characters would have had pointed ears, which would conflict with the standard Vulcan makeup. For Jennifer Lien, the actress cast to play the role of Kes, the makeup department created a larger but totally different style of rounded ears and designed a slightly wider jaw appliance. In this way, Jennifer's natural looks were allowed to come

through. By creating a new style of ear for the Ocampans, the makeup department was also able to fabricate a large variety of ears for the different Ocampans, both male and female, who appeared on *Voyager*.

Jennifer Lien as Kes.

The producers wanted an alien who was very likable, very toylike, but ultimately almost huggable.

MIKE WESTMORE ON THE TALAXIANS

Mr. Neelix was the last character we designed for *Voyager,* saved for the very end because the studio believed that Neelix would be one of the most merchandizable characters in the series because of his looks. The producers wanted an alien who was very likable, very toy-like, ultimately almost huggable. At the time Neelix was designed, *The Lion King* was playing in theaters and as I watched the animated feature, I became enthralled with the look of the animals, especially the colorings. I thought that description of Neelix that we'd gotten from the producers could be enhanced with the look of a friendly cartoon animal. So we took the aspect of the animals and adapted them to the look of the Talaxians.

I designed him the way I would a "Westmore alien" in that I gave him a tough rowdiness by designing a wig for him out of goat hair and spiky meerkat eyebrows. Then I gave him a cutesy, non-Trekkie look by rounding out his face so he would be completely non-threatening. In direct contrast to the pointed Klingon, meat-eating, flesh-tearing fangs, I rounded off Neelix's teeth and flattened out the chewing surfaces so he'd look like a leaf-eater. Pointy teeth are scary, rounded teeth are friendly; at least that's how humans perceive animals. We added the spots to give him an alien look while the wig and the muttonchops come from the warthog character.

MICHAEL WESTMORE ON THE BORG, SEVEN OF NINE, THE BORG QUEEN, AND ONE

It was the movie *First Contact* that completely changed the look of the Borg. Initially, because the Borg heads were encased in a helmet that was prepainted, the only thing makeup had to do was the facial makeup. The tubing, the attachments, and the hand appliances with the Borg tools were all prefabricated and had only to be fitted in place. This made the makeup job relatively simple and took only half an hour to complete. But *First Contact*, with its more elaborate outfitting of the Borg, changed all that and affected us a great deal, because we couldn't bring the old version back after the more elaborate Borg had made their appearance in the feature. We had to use the *First Contact* Borg and these took about five hours to complete, dressing and makeup combined. By the sixth season of *Voyager*, we got it down to four hours.

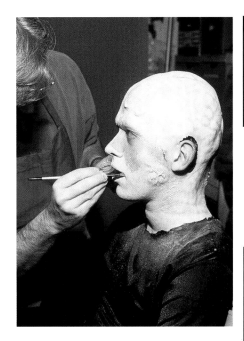

Bradley Look transforms an actor into a Borg.
R. Haney

The edges of the appliance are airbrushed to blend with the base makeup.
R. Haney

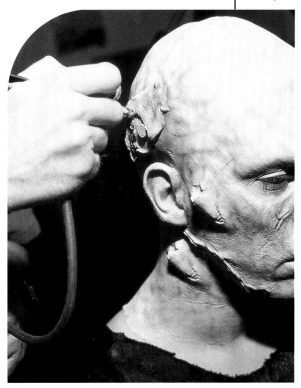

Top, left: Larger pieces of Borg technology/appliances are left for last.
Top, right: Hoses and other Borg features are connected to predetermined spots.
Bottom: Another touch of the airbrush to the base makeup.

All photos R. Haney

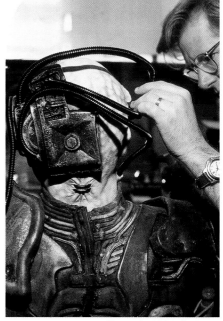

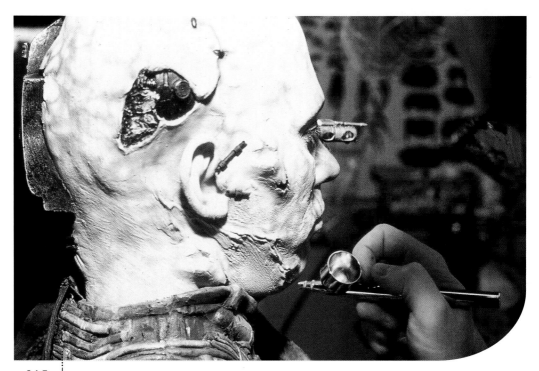

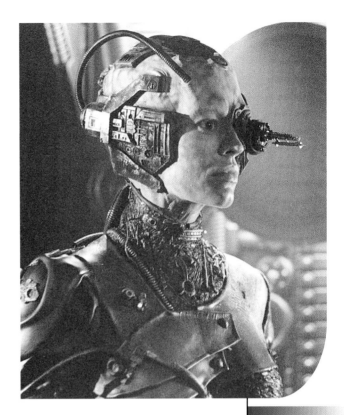

SEVEN OF NINE

When she was a Borg, Seven of Nine was indistinguishable from the rest of the Borg insofar as her initial makeup was concerned. But after she joined *Voyager*, makeup developed her own exclusive design. We got the Borg eye off of her as quickly as we could. Once the eye came off, she was more recognizable as a human. The rest of her makeup was changed so that all that remained of her Borg costume were two facial implants and the hand implant. We brought her coloring back right away and got rid of the bald cap so she looked human.

THE BORG QUEEN

The first Borg Queen on *Voyager* was an improvement on the queen from *First Contact* in that the electronics on her head were different. She has the same head shape and cheeks as she did in the movie, but the front of the throat is different and

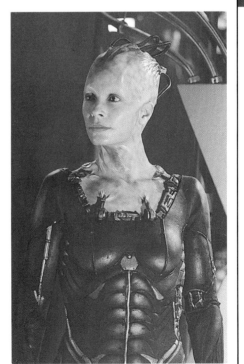

Top, left:
Severed from the hive mind of the Borg.
Robbie Robinson

Top, right:
Jeri Ryan as the fully assimilated Seven of Nine.
Robbie Robinson

Left: The makeup for *Voyager*'s Borg Queen, Susanne Thompson, differs from that of her feature film counterpart. Her electronics are on the exterior, while they were buried in the headpiece in the film.
Michael Yarish

Opposite:
Alice Krige as
the Borg Queen
in *First Contact*.
You can see her
"blinkies" in this
photo.
Elliott Marks

Left:
J. Paul Boehmer
as One.
Ron Tom

makes her look as if she has corrugated tubing running down her throat. The electronic piece on the back of her head has running lights on it. She reappears in the two-parter (ending Season 6 and beginning Season 7) with the exact same makeup when *Voyager* is again attacked by the Borg and Janeway, Torres, and Tuvok are captured.

ONE

This twenty-ninth-century Borg had to be modified somewhat from the Borg that had been encountered in the Delta Quadrant. He had a special neon eyepiece instead of blinking LEDs, a reduced number of tubes to reflect the advanced Borg technology, a different lighting system for his suit, and a special Borg-type appliance that covered his right ear. We used a small two-inch neon light for his eye that had to be constructed large enough for the neon fixture and to accommodate the wires running from the appliance to a battery pack on his back. The other Borg appliances were smoother and the color tones were bluer.

Dawson's and Russ's Borg makeup leaves the new drones recognizable as Torres and Tuvok.

Michael Yarish

As frightening as this vision of an assimilated Janeway is, the makeup was created to imply that there were still more horrors that the Borg could perform on the captain.

Michael Yarish

THE VOYAGER BORG

In the final scene at the cutaway at the end of Season 6, we have the very beginnings of the Borgification process for Janeway, Torres, and Tuvok. They don't have the major tubes yet or any of the eyepieces. They've already become bald and there are a few implants on their heads. And their coloring has not yet gone all the way to Borg dead pale.

CAPTAIN PROTON

Captain Proton and the rest of the cast of the holonovel were a combination of the hairstyles, makeup, wardrobe, and props from the 1930s Flash Gordon and Buck Rogers serials. The makeup department had to re-create the style of 1930s motion picture makeup to achieve an authentic look. The designers used heavy liners around the eyes, a heavy makeup base for the actors, and researched the way black-and-white makeup was used in combination with the harsh lighting of the period to create very stark shadows to convey drama and mood. The heavy makeup and hairstyling, when combined with the props and costumes of the period, created the look.

Left: Martin Rayner as Doctor Chaotica.
Ron Tom

Above: The highlights on Mulgrew's face were over-applied to enhance her features and ensure they will show in black-and-white.
Ron Tom

THE KAZON

The producers wanted a character for the launch of the *Voyager* series who would fill the role of the Klingons, but would be clearly not Klingons. They had to be cruel and barbaric, without the sense of honor of the Klingons—destroyers, not warriors. Makeup took a forehead based on an almost devilish structure, and the comb that runs down the forehead was taken from the look of the vulture's neck. In subsequent episodes, the makeup department took the vulture neck from the Kazon comb and built an appliance for the Kazon neck. In addition, makeup created a new

Anthony DeLongis as the Kazon Jal Culluh.
Bryon J. Cohen

nose tip that lengthened the actors' noses and added spikes coming out from below the nostrils. To distinguish them even further from the Klingons, the makeup department colored the Kazon a burnt orange instead of a deep brown.

THE HIROGEN

This design was based on the gila monster, which consisted of small beading that became consistently larger as it ran up the face toward the crown of the skull. Hirogen were very tall characters, so the producers cast the largest actors they could find to play the roles, one of whom was at least seven feet tall. This meant that the heads created by the makeup department had to be oversized and required a whole new sizing of the props the Hirogen would have to carry.

TUVIX

This transporter hybrid of Tuvok and Neelix was shaded lighter than Tuvok but darker than Neelix and had smaller versions of pointed Vulcan ears built onto a Neelix head.

TOM PARIS "THRESHOLD" ALIEN

This character was based on a salamander, but there were a lot of opticals, because Paris went through a series of transformations. The makeup department created stages of the makeup to reflect Tom Paris's mutation into the reptile, and the artists added more bumps to his changing head with every progress point. A set of contact lenses was created for Bobby McNeill to wear at the final stage of the change. They also had him rinse his mouth with a mouthwash made out of blue dye to emphasize his transformation.

THE VIDIIANS

These were creatures who suffered from a disease called the phage. Accordingly, they prolong their lives by seeking transplants from any life-form. Makeup designed the Vidiians as if they were patchwork quilts, built out of harvested organs and body parts to replace those that were consumed by the disease. To make the Vidiians walking montages of the creatures whose skin they grafted on, the department used the skin designs from previous aliens, patches of Talaxian spots here or an orange Kazon patch there to reinforce the image of the Vidiians as bioscavengers of the Delta Quadrant.

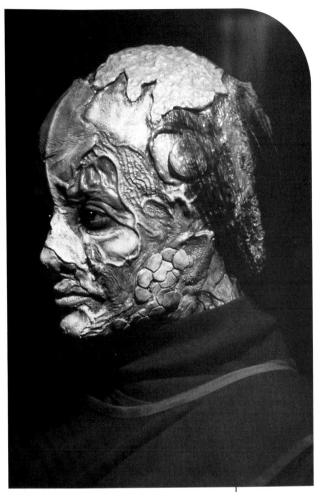

THE MALONS OR THE "GARBAGE PAIL MEN"

Especially heavyset actors were hired, and their faces were then used as the bases for the appliances to turn into very round, pudgy demeanors. They wore nose, forehead, lower lip, and cheek appliances instead of full heads and had lots of hair but with hairlines pulled back to show that it was thinning. They were made up with very dirty-looking teeth, and their bodies were coated with makeup to look like dirt, sweat, and grease.

TOVA VEER OF THE VOTH

This character was based on a full dinosaur head and face to which was added a special set of dentures and contact lenses. Each character of the Voth had his own special head, gloves, and dentures.

TREVIS

This character from a holonovel was created out of a full head, contact lenses painted a wood grain, and little stumps glued onto his fingertips. Similarly, Flotter the water character had a pair of contact lenses painted to look like water.

Left: Ken Magee as Controller Emck.
Paul McCullum

Above: Susan Diol as Denara Pel.
Robbie Robinson

Above:
Henry Woronicz as
Forra Gegen and
Christopher Liam
Moore as Tova Veer.
Robbie Robinson

Left:
Justin Lewis
as Trevis.
Danny Feld

Right:
Wallace Langham
as Flotter.
Danny Feld

PRALOR AUTOMATED PERSONAL UNIT

The robots that Torres encountered who attempted to force her to build one of their "species" were created out of separate vacu-formed components that were fitted over the actors to allow them full movement and flexibility.

THE KAAKONIANS

The members of this aggressive race were responsible for the destruction of the Talaxian civilization when they bombarded the moon Rinax with a metron cascade. The characters' makeup consisted of heavy eyebrow appliances with ridges running up the sides of their temples to the hairline, a sharp appliance over the ridge of the nose, and a chin piece.

LEONARDO DA VINCI

John Rhys-Davies played the Renaissance master. His makeup consisted of a da Vinci–style nose appliance and a special beard, mustache and eyebrows.

Above, left:
Rick Worthy as
Pralor Automated
Personal Unit 3947.
Robbie Robinson

Above, right:
James Sloyan
as Doctor Jetrel.
Robbie Robinson

Left:
John Rhys-Davies
as Leonardo da Vinci.
Robbie Robinson

...I brought with me a sense that a prop not only had to look like the real thing but had to be handled like the real thing on camera.

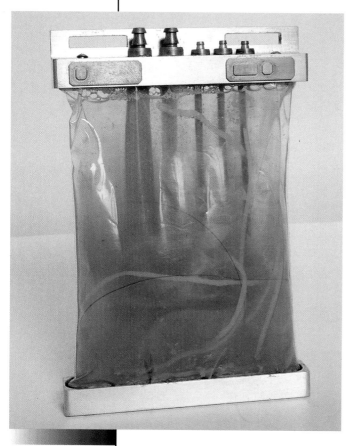

Robbie Robinson

Opposite: It's just a prop, there's nothing real about this type-3 phaser. But the look of the prop and the actor's body language make the threat believable.

Ron Tom

ALAN SIMS ON *VOYAGER* PROPS

Our challenge from *TNG* right through *Voyager* was to advance the technology. We succeeded in *TNG* and succeeded even more so in *DS9*, creating an environment where the Starfleet props and alien props could blend visually on the same screen. But this had raised the bar so much higher that we had to create even more of an advanced look because the *Starship Voyager* was a scientific exploration ship.

Weapons

By *Voyager*, we had evolved that look into what I call the "boomerang" type-2 phaser with the sharply curved handle and contoured to conform closer to the hip. This was a design that had evolved from the straight handle in the first season of *TNG*.

The next phaser design we modified was the type-3, the phaser rifle. Rick Sternbach and I designed a new weapon called the compression phaser, which looks like a far more lethal weapon than the older type-3. It's sleeker and larger and "holds" its power in two casings along the side and, in the collective imagination of the *Star Trek* designers, packs a stronger punch than the older weapon. And the weapon design fit my basic specification that it had to be fabricated out of metal and look like it was just one unit of millions of identical units manufactured for Starfleet.

Metal phasers are important as a prop not just because of the look. They're important because they're heavier, have heft, and force the actors to handle them as if they're real. If you look at the original series, you'll see moments where it's obvious that something the actor is lifting is nothing more than plastic or cardboard. The actor raises it too easily or swings the weapon to fire with no impression that this is a real device. When I came to *TNG*, I brought with me a sense that a prop not only had to look like the real thing but had to be handled like the real thing on camera. So when it came to designing phasers and phaser rifles, I wanted them made out of metal so the actor would

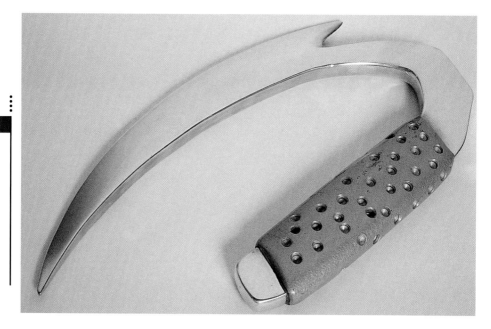

have to treat it like a real weapon. I carried this to *Voyager*, where I wanted the weapons not only to look heavier, but to feel heavier in the actors' hands.

The props also have to be durable because they get a lot of wear and tear on the set. People who watch television don't realize that during a shoot, a weakly made prop can simply snap off at key joint points and shut down an entire shoot while the crew runs around to replace it. That's why the equipment and weapons that I have built have to stand the stress test so they won't break on camera and don't have to be handled as if they will break. So I have them built out of aluminum wherever possible or cast out of fiberglass so that they're strong and actors don't have to baby them. Having heavier weapon props also means that I have to train the actor in physically handling the device, rehearsing them with it, so that it doesn't look like he or she has never used the weapon before. We go through firing and defensive postures so that they look like they know what to do with a weapon.

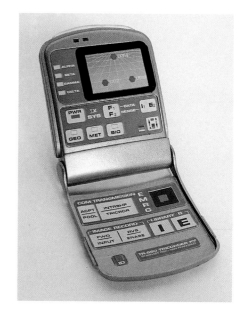

Scanning and Transcribing Devices

The *Voyager* tricorders are completely different from the *TNG* tricorders. We came up with a smaller, sleeker design that was conceived not by our Art Department but from an outside design shop, and the producers liked the look and adopted it.

Medical Apparatus

I designed the medical apparatus for *Voyager* by foraging around electronics shops, Sav-On and Thrift drugstores, household stores, and places where I could find interesting shapes I could convert into something that would look like an instrument. For example, temperature gauges, soil testers, garage-door remotes, and electronic continuity testers all make great medical instruments. On *TNG*, we spent money to design these things. But I found that if you walk into an electronics store, the equipment they have, especially the testing equipment, looks more high-tech and futuristic than anything we can design on paper and try to get manufactured for us.

The cortical stimulators and neural devices the Doctor uses are simple devices held in place by double-edge tape that's very thin and very sticky so that it can't be seen on camera. Because the tape is so sticky, it adheres immediately to any object it touches. So, if you notice, when the cortical stimulator or

other device is set on a medical tray, it's always at a slight angle so the tape won't adhere. Then when the Doctor or Paris picks it up, he always holds the taped backing away from the camera so the audience won't see it. It's a kind of sleight of hand to make the prop work.

Borg Props

All the arms for the Borg after the motion picture *First Contact* were designed by Todd Masters. Also after the feature, we replaced the little remote-controlled servo motors with cables and rings inside the

The beginning
stages of a bike
assimilation.
Alan Sims

arm so the Borg actors could turn the tools on and off by themselves. We turned a completely electronic radio-controlled device into a mechanical one run by a simple cable.

Borg Bikes

One of the devices that really stood out on *Voyager* was the Borg bicycle that we created for one of the Borg children in "Child's Play." When the producers said they wanted an interpretation of a bicycle for the twenty-fourth century, I looked around as hard as I could for some type of design that wouldn't look like today's bike but would nevertheless convey the image of a bicycle. So after calling around and coming up with zeroes everywhere I went I finally went to a high-end bike store in Los Angeles and saw the exact model I was looking for. I just needed to open up my brain to design ideas because I knew the prop was going to be a key element

of the Borg children episode. Suddenly, there in the corner was a bike called the "California Chariot," and I knew I had found what I was looking for.

This bike was the most bizarre device I'd ever seen, a bike you didn't sit on at all: a front wheel, a set of handlebars, but the back end had two runners you stood on like two separate skateboards spread a foot and a half apart. It's like a pair of scooters in back attached to a bicycle front end. You stand on it and scoot with one foot or the other while you steer with your hands. I knew I could cosmetically transform this device into what we needed. The best part about this bike was that they had several sizes there, arranged according to the age of the rider. There was everything from adult to kiddie versions of the bike. So I snapped off a couple of Polaroid shots for the producers, bought the bike, and took it back to the lot.

The producers loved the concept when

I explained what I wanted to do. HMS Creative Productions started by putting a fairing over the front wheel to cover up the spokes and then they replaced the straight handlebars with two independent handlebars, one for the left and one for the right, that came directly off the wheel, and finally they put on some more fairings to cover up other parts of the frame and took off the logos to change the look of the bike. This bike spent about three minutes, or three script pages, on camera and was very successful.

Captain Proton Props

The props for Captain Proton were delivered to me in a full five-act treatment in which I could see what the look and feel of the characters had to be. I remembered the Flash Gordon serials. I honed in on exactly what was required in the script such as the hand ray gun; Satan's Robot, which came right out of the Commando Cody episodes; and the Commando Cody rocket pack. After I found the black-and-white stills from those episodes, I showed them to the producers, who agreed that this was the robot we wanted. So wardrobe built the costume.

The back jet pack itself also came from the research pictures of the Commando Cody. A friend of mine who is a Cody fan built the pack for me and found where the original actor from the Cody serials was doing autograph signings and showed him the photos of what he was building. Finally he showed up at a Cody signing dressed in a Commando Cody outfit and the actor who had portrayed him in serials looked at him and was absolutely shocked. Tears came to the actor's eyes because it brought back so many memories. Then we hired an effects company to provide the Chaotica devices, the Tesla machines, the Dr. Frankenstein static electricity rods, and the Death Ray. The entire ambience

Robert Duncan McNeill as Captain Proton. Hard to say who enjoyed the role-playing more, the actor or the character.
Paul McCullum

of the lab was so accurate you'd think Lawrence Talbot would show up in the scene begging you to lock him up before the full moon rose and he'd become the Wolfman. Unfortunately, the machinery on the set was so loud that you couldn't hear the dialogue, so we had to blend the two scenes optically.

ing the makeup department, I create a side arm and whatever other prop may be involved for this race to complement the picture of the race on camera.

Another aspect of alien weapons and props is that each prop we create has to be the prototype of itself because we have no time to test these things out. We

Alien Props and Weapons

Part of what I have to do when I first see a script with aliens in it is to ask the producers what the backgrounds of these aliens are. Are they basketweavers or hunters, ship traders, carnivores, or plant foragers? This is important because when you develop a weapon it has to fit how the script says these aliens live. Then I check with wardrobe to see how they're outfitting the race. Do they wear long flowing robes or body armor, uniforms or individualized items of clothing? Once I've coordinated with everybody, includ-

have to make sure not only that the look will be right, but that the prop will hold up on camera when handled by actors who can't treat them as delicate objects.

Kazon Weapons

These were crude, yet futuristic, weapons that had to convey the barbarism of the Kazon. These rifles and pistols looked antiquated even though they're twenty-fourth-century. I used copper tubing and bent copper joints that ran to a barrel-head that was a different shape than the phaser rifle. The copper tubing became

the body of the unit itself and was attached to a leather strap over a wood-looking grip that had a completely different presentation. It actually looked like a plumbing nightmare, but the prop worked because it helped define the Kazons.

Hirogen Weapons

As barbaric as the Hirogen were, they were different from the Kazon because the Hirogen were trophy hunters who, although they competed with one another, were nevertheless rule-driven. There was an organization to their violence that differed from the tribalism of the Kazon.

The Hirogen were very large people, overpoweringly large. In the very first episode we hired actors that were close to seven feet and then put platforms in their boots to give them even greater height. That meant that these guys couldn't wield props built for humans; they had to be oversized props, large weapons the size of bazookas that would take two normal-sized humans to deploy. So their phaser rifles had to be huge and heavy. I got the idea from comic books and had a production company expand on the design, and it created a phaser rifle that looked like a tank killer. On the top of the weapon, I added a viewing panel that looked like a

heads-up cockpit display in today's planes. This panel threw up a dot display that looked like a heat-seeking targeting system to help them identify the signatures of their prey. The weapon also had a light source

Robbie Robinson

to penetrate the dark areas where they hunted. It had a lot of electronics on it, different modes of activation to make it seem as if these were not just phasers but complete weapons systems that allowed the Hirogen to survive and succeed in the most dangerous environments.

We only had ten days to create this intense prop. The body of this unit was vacu-formed and then sanded and shaped and electroplated so that it had a metallic chrome, cold steel look. We then built in the electronics and the battery pack. When it was all done in the shop, I brought these two weapons onto the lot to show to the producers. They said, "It's so big." I told them, "You said you wanted this thing to be gargantuan." And when they saw it in the hands of the seven-foot-two actors, they knew they had the right look.

Twenty-ninth Century Gadgetry

For twenty-ninth-century props, we developed a tricorder that was half the size of our tricorder, because the vision of the future was things are smaller. The phaser was a strange-looking weapon with no barrel or orifice. Its power was stored in

the front of the weapon. And it had to make the people of the twenty-fourth century stand in awe of it.

Spider Props

One of my favorite props involved creating the spiders for the *Voyager* episode "Gravity," in which the crew discovers a young woman who catches spiders and eats them for sustenance. Not only did I have to research many types of spiders for this prop, but once I found an insect design that I liked, I modified it with a series of warts and blemishes and then had it built in the prop shop I use. Then I went to a garden store and modified a gardener's three-pronged hand rake by straightening out the angle and turning it into a weapon. I took off the plastic handle and had a piece of metal turned so that it was now a steel hunting tool.

CHAPTER EIGHT

How to Create Your Own Aliens & Artifacts

Star Trek's lasting popularity has always resided in its imaginative representations of alien life and the technologies of the twenty-third and twenty-fourth centuries. But these representations are the work of twentieth- and twenty-first-century artists and designers using today's tools and techniques. In this chapter we want to show you how you can apply some of the techniques and materials we used to create your own versions of Star Trek aliens and the props. We'll start with makeup.

For the makeup kits in this section we want to thank Doug Morton from Rubies for supplying us with the *Star Trek* character makeup kits and costumes. We also want to thank Dana Nye from the Ben Nye makeup company for supplying the cosmetics used to create the Data and Seven of Nine makeups. Kari Beth Rust from the Illinois State University Theater Department also helped by providing the additional costumes for the photo shoot, and Gary Walters was the photographer

Data

1 Model Clayton Stang before makeup.

As with all makeup application, Clayton starts with a clean, dry face.

2 Clayton slicks back his hair using a hair gel such as Dep and combs his hair off his face. Dry hair in place using a hair dryer on low or cool setting.

Use a temporary hair color, such as Ben Nye's Midnight Black (MB-1), if your natural hair color is too light. Follow the directions on the bottle. *Note: always check temporary color on a small strand of your hair before general application. Keep the product out of your eyes.*

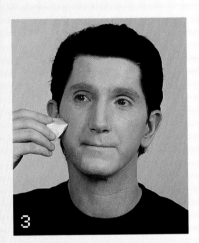 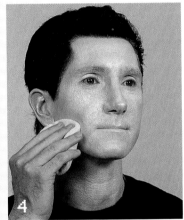 

3 Next, Clayton applies Ben Nye Ultra Matte Foundation (CN-0) to his entire face and neck using a cosmetic latex sponge. Also, don't forget the ears. Pat or stipple the base so that there are no streaks. It should appear completely even.

4 The cream base is set with Ben Nye Lumiere Luxe Powder. The Data setting powder is a mix of Iced Gold (LX-2 with a small addition of Aztec Gold (LX-3). This is worked into the makeup using a velour powder puff.

Dust off the excess powder using a powder brush, taking great care not to get powder in your eyes or hair.

5 Next, Clayton uses a Ben Nye MagiColor cream liner pencil Black (MC-1) to sketch on the pointed sideburns with small strokes. An alternate method is to hand-lay the painted sideburns using crepe wool and spirit gum adhesive. Consult the "sideburn bible" chart for the proper placement, pg. 156.

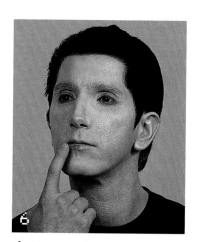

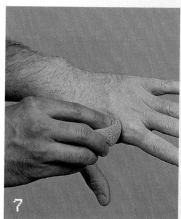

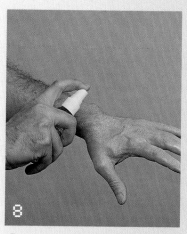

6 Now apply a *small* amount of Ben Nye Fireworks Bronze (FW-11) to the lips to cover all pink areas.

7 Using a damp Hydra sponge (HS-1), apply a mixture of Ben Nye Cake Makeup Light Ivory (PC-02) with a small amount of MagiCake Aqua Paint Maize (LA-89) to the tops of the hands. Powder with the same Lumiere Lux Powder as used on the face. *Note: instead of using water to moisten the sponge, try using Ben Nye LiquiSet (MLB-11) to give your hand makeup a more resistant finish.*

8 Set the hand makeup afterward using Ben Nye Final Seal (FY-2). Allow to dry and repeat a second application.

9 Here's Data in his deluxe-quality *Star Trek: The Next Generation* tunic, available from Rubies.

Klingon

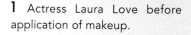

1 Actress Laura Love before application of makeup.

2 Laura has removed all of her street makeup and has washed and dried her face. We begin by placing a nylon wig cap over her head to keep her hair away from her face.

Laura tries on the headpiece from the Rubies deluxe *Star Trek: The Next Generation* Klingon character kit to check the general fit. If the headpiece covers your ears, mark with a makeup pencil where your ear holes are. Remove the headpiece to cut a small hole on each side where you've marked the headpiece to allow you to hear properly. If the headpiece is too large, you can glue a section of foam into the top of the head-piece using contact cement (available in most hardware stores and supermarkets). *Note: never use scissors to trim or cut the headpiece while you are wearing it. Always use a makeup pencil first, then remove the headpiece and cut.*

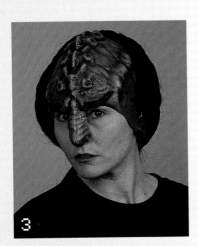

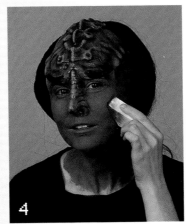

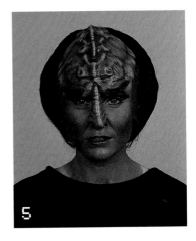

3 Now that the headpiece has been customized, Laura has slipped it back on. You can either use the double-faced theatrical tape to fix the nose in place, or use the spirit gum that is also included in the kit. If you choose the spirit gum, paint a thin layer on the sides of your nose. Allow the glue to become sticky, which will take approximately three to five minutes.

4 Laura has applied the specially formulated Klingon base to the rest of her face. She has carried the makeup down her neck as well.

5 Laura has applied a second coat of base to create more shadows. For men, you should avoid applying the makeup to your upper lip and chin where your mustache and goatee will be applied. Men: apply spirit gum to the upper lip and chin and allow three to five minutes to become sticky before applying facial hair pieces.

Laura Love as Lursa or B'Etor from the house of Duras wearing the Rubies Klingon Female costume.

Ferengi Starfleet Science Officer

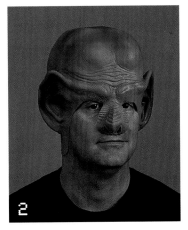

1 John Poole before applying makeup.

John has washed and dried his face and is giving himself a once-over shave to remove any light stubble.

2 John tries on the headpiece from the Rubies deluxe *Star Trek: Deep Space Nine* Ferengi character kit to check the general fit and make sure the headpiece did not interfere with his vision. If it interferes with yours, you should trim the area around the eyes after you remove the headpiece. Also make sure that the nostrils on the Ferengi nose are adequately open for normal breathing. If not, remove the headpiece and use cuticle scissors to trim carefully any unwanted latex. *Note: if the headpiece has any dents in the latex you can remove them by using a hair dryer on a hot setting and waving it around inside the headpiece. Use extreme caution when doing this so as not to burn your fingers or the surface of the latex. Another method is to stuff the inside of the headpiece with clean, nonprinted paper to force the dents out.*

You can also use cotton batting.

John has applied his headpiece and has attached his Ferengi nose either with the theatrical tape or with the spirit gum. If you decide to use spirit gum, make sure to paint a thin layer on the sides of your nose and allow three to five minutes for it to become sticky before applying the nosepiece.

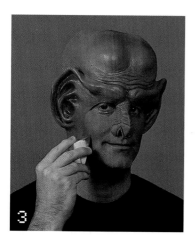

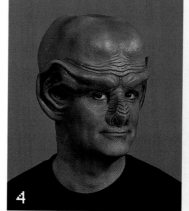

3 John uses one of the sponges supplied with the kit to apply the specially formulated Ferengi base onto the rest of his face. He uses a stippling or patting motion so that the base has an even, smooth look.

4 Though not included in the Rubies kit, you can further accent the Ferengi appearance by using a darker theatrical cream make-up to create shadows.

Next, using soap and water, John cleans the Ferengi teeth that are included in the kit. Making sure to rinse well—this avoids ingesting soap. The teeth have been designed to conform to both the upper and lower gums. John holds the teeth together to determine which is the upper. The "overbite" section fits his upper gum. He inserts the teeth in his mouth to check fit. He'll remove and trim, if necessary, any excess latex using cuticle scissors.

While no tooth adhesive is required, if you wish to wear the teeth for a prolonged period, we recommend you first chew a piece of sugarless gum until it is soft. Then place the chewing gum inside the teeth and press down onto your own gum. The teeth are designed to adhere to your gums, not to your own teeth. You can also use commercially available dental adhesives for this purpose, but be sure to follow the manufacturer's recommended instructions if you decide to apply the Ferengi teeth in this fashion.

5 Using a Hydra Sponge (HS-1) from Ben Nye, John applies a mixture of Cake Foundation Tan No. 2 (PC-11) and MagiCake Aqua Paint Bright Orange (LA-17) to his hands. After this dries, set using Ben Nye Final Seal (FY-2), and then apply blue nail polish.

6 John in the finished makeup. He can also attach the Ferengi headpiece to the back of his head by gluing a section of fabric to the back of his head using contact cement. John is wearing a *Deep Space Nine* Science Officer's tunic from Rubies.

The Borg (Third of Five)

1 Matt Steffen before assimilation by the Borg.

Matt washes his face and pats it dry.

Matt is using Rubies deluxe *Star Trek: The Next Generation* Borg character kit. He will have to make some custom adjustments for his size, the instructions for which are included in the kit. Besides these suggestions, you can also personalize your Borg costume helmet by cutting up the back of the helmet with scissors, then using contact cement to attach a section of Velcro to the two sides. This was the process we used with Matt to make it easier for him to slip on the helmet after the finish of the base makeup application.

2 Matt tries on the headpiece so that he can see where the border of the inside of the helmet fits around his skin. Using a black makeup stick, he traces around the edge. The facial tube circular plug is also outlined. Next Matt removes the headpiece.

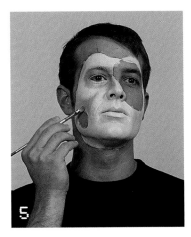

3 Matt applies the Hugh-style eyepiece over his left eye so that he can trace around the outside edge.

4 With helmet and eyepiece outlined, Matt applies white cream makeup, which comes with the kit, carefully patting it onto the face except in those areas where the eyepiece and circular plug are to be glued. Keep applying the makeup until the color looks smooth and even.

5 Next, Matt mixes a little black color with some white to make a gray color for shadows. He then applies this, lightly patting around the right eye, then over the right temple and in the hollow of his cheeks for a cadaverous look. Again, avoid getting any makeup in those areas where the appliances are to be glued.

6 Matt applies a small amount of black makeup to his left eyelid and under the left eye. This step will help hide the eye so that it is not easily detectable through the hologram of the eyepiece.

7 Matt has slipped on his helmet. He applies spirit gum carefully on the skin where the eyepiece will go, allows it three to five minutes to become sticky, and then presses the eyepiece in place. You must exercise extreme caution so as not to get any spirit gum in your eye. Now Matt applies spirit gum to glue the tubes in place.

8 Resistance was futile:
Matt has been transformed
into a Borg. For the complete
assimilation, you will want to
create a black Borg costume
out of a tight black sweatshirt
with tubes glued to various
spots and a black glove with
various Dremel tools attached
such as a tiny saw or drill.

Romulan

1 Elizabeth Mullenix before her transformation into a Romulan intelligence officer. She will use the Rubies Romulan makeup kit.

Having freshly cleaned and dried her face, Elizabeth pins back her hair and slips on a nylon wig cap.

2 She has glued her latex ear tips on using spirit gum. First, you have to prefit your ear tips to make sure they are seated at the proper angle. Check how your ears fit against the photos of Romulans in the earlier chapters.

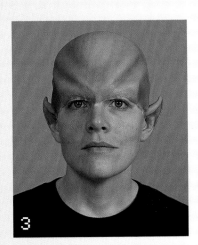

3 Elizabeth has prefitted her Romulan forehead piece to see if she needed to trim away any latex. She marked the excess areas with a makeup pencil prior to removal so she knows where to trim. After customizing it for her head size, she removes the headpiece and the ears and uses spirit gum on the inside edge of the appliance and on the ear tips to glue them onto her forehead and ears.

4 Now she applies specially formulated Romulan base makeup to the rest of her face and neck, using one of the sponges included in the Rubies kit.

5 Though it is not included in the Rubies kit, Elizabeth applies eye shadow and cheek shading to accent her Romulan look even further.

6 For her final appearance in finished makeup, Elizabeth has glued her eyebrows into place using spirit gum. As in all applications, she paints a thin layer of spirit gum onto the appliance and waits three to five minutes for it to become sticky. Then she applies the eyebrows at an upward angle from the bridge of her nose to her temples. She then applies a deep red or near violet lipstick, then puts on her wig, spraying it lightly with hairspray to take care of any fly-away ends. The intelligence officer cape and hood were provided by the Illinois State University costume shop.

Vulcan

1 Our model Clayton Stang before makeup.

2 Clayton has cleaned and dried his face and placed his hair under a nylon wig cap. Next he tries on his ears for the proper angle. Then he uses spirit gum to glue them on.

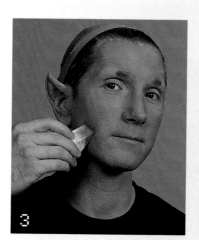

3 Now Clayton glues latex "blenders" over half of his eyebrows using spirit gum. Then he uses one of the sponges included in the Rubies Vulcan kit to apply the specially formulated Vulcan makeup onto his entire face. The base is blended down onto his neck, as well as onto the uncovered portion of his ears.

4 Clayton has glued on his eyebrows using spirit gum. Then he applies a little extra eye shadow and cheek shading to accent the makeup. Eye shadow and shading makeup is not included in the kit.

5 Final touches include the application of the Vulcan wig approximately the width of three fingers above the bridge of the nose. He then makes up his hands using a mixture of Ben Nye's Cake Foundation Chinese (PC-43) and MagiColor Aqua Paint Marigold (CF-10), and the makeup is then set using Ben Nye Final Seal (FV-2). The costume, a white tunic, hood, and cape, was provided by the Illinois State University costume shop.

Seven of Nine

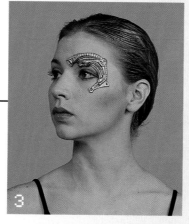

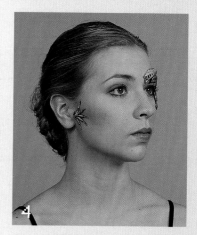

1 Actress Brenda Hogan as Annika Hansen as she might look today had she not been assimilated by the Borg when she was a child.

2 After cleaning and drying her face and pulling back her hair, Brenda applies Ben Nye Matte Foundation Shinsei Fair (SH-2) as the base color. Next, she uses Mellow Orange Lite (MO-11) as an under-eye concealer. She next applies Creme Shadow Medium Brown (CS-2) under her cheekbones for highlight and to accentuate her natural features. She sets the makeup using Fair Translucent

(TP-1) face power and Powder Blusher Nectar Peach (PB-22) to her cheekbones. She uses Ben Nye pressed eye shadow Taupe (ES-34) and Bark (ES-60) on her eyelids. Brenda also applies a lip conditioner to her lips before lining them with lip pencil Spice (LP-35).

3 Brenda glues the Borg eyepiece over her left eyebrow using spirit gum.

4 And now she glues the Borg wheel in front of her right ear.

5 Here is Brenda in the completed Seven of Nine makeup. Her hand piece was slipped over her left hand and glued where necessary using spirit gum. Her *Voyager* communicator pin was provided by Rubies and her costume was provided by the Illinois State University costume shop.

Masks

If you'd rather not apply your makeup yourself, you can purchase your favorite *Star Trek* character as an overhead mask, also available from Rubies.

Originally the Don Post Mask Company manufactured a line of masks based on the original series, featuring Captain Kirk and Mr. Spock masks cast directly from the life masks of William Shatner and Leonard Nimoy. The Captain Kirk mask was released in a standard flesh-tone paint with light brown crepe wool for hair. A copy of that same mask was purchased by director John Carpenter and repainted a solid white and worn by "The Shape" in his 1979 horror film *Halloween*. The same mask was used in the 1981 sequel.

In addition to Kirk and Spock, the Don Post Company also made the M-113 Creature or the Salt Vampire, Gorn, and the horned Mugato. After the release of *Star Trek: The Motion Picture*, the Don Post Company manufactured not only a Mr. Spock mask, but the bald-headed Vulcan Master and the Klingon Captain.

Rubies has not only the Kirk and Spock masks, but Quark, Odo, Cardassians, Worf, a Borg, Data, Picard, Geordi La Forge, and Neelix.

Props

THE SIMS BEACON

The wrist flashlight that came to be known as the Sims beacon has been one of the most successful props on *Voyager*, replacing the palm-held light that was used on *TNG*. Modeled after the way police and federal officers hold their flashlights, the Sims beacon is simply a powerful light that's attached to the user's wrist, freeing both hands. You can make your own Sims beacon very easily with two mini flashlights such as the Lumalite Light Force model and a black wraparound wristband such as the Tru-Fit. You can find the Lumalites at Thrift or Sav-On drug stores or hardware stores and the Tru-Fit at any sporting-goods store or in the athletic bandage section of a large drug store.

Simply wrap the wrist band around either your right or left wrist, insert the flashlights between the layers of the bandage, making sure they're firmly in place, and turn them on. Now you have a Sims beacon for under $15.

ALAN SIMS ON BUILDING A DERMAL REGENERATOR

One of the most challenging parts of being a property master is coming up with the medical instruments for sickbay. Often a script will refer to a medical device, such as a dermal regenerator, as if it's already in existence when, in fact, no one knows what it's supposed to look like. If you're lucky on a particular episode, the Art Department will have come up with a preliminary sketch, but the working prototype is usually the job of the property master to create.

The dermal regenerator does exactly what its name implies: it heals bruises, cuts, and minor skin injuries by regenerating human tissue. To make your own dermal regenerator at home you will need: an electric hairbrush, available at upscale drugstores, a 3" to 4" piece of acrylic tubing from a household-goods store, two red LEDs and a small resistor, which you can get at Radio Shack or another electronics store, sandpaper in fine and coarse grades, and tools such as a Dremel, a circular saw, an electric drill, and a pencil soldering iron. This is not a job for a first-timer because it involves the use of cutting tools and a soldering iron, which can be dangerous if you don't know how to use one.

Step 1

Make sure the switch to the electric hairbrush is in the off position and remove the batteries from the handle. Next, lay the brush on a workbench and, with a small screwdriver, gently pry away the two rubber O-rings that hold the two halves of the handle together. One O-ring is near the base of the U-shaped brace and the other is at the base of the handle.

Step 2

Once the O-rings have been removed, you can now use your screwdriver to separate the two halves of the brush and lay them on your workbench side by side.

Step 3

Using your Dremel tool with the cutting blade, cut out the center section of the brush head completely so as to remove the brush and bristles and expose the natural U-shape of the unit.

Dermal Regenerator S.T. VOYAGER

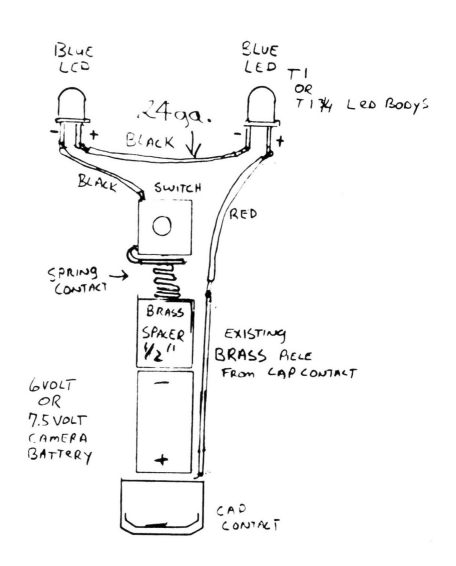

BLUE LCD

BLUE LED T1 OR T1¾ LED BODYS

.24ga.

BLACK ↓

BLACK

SWITCH

RED

SPRING CONTACT →

BRASS SPACER ½"

EXISTING BRASS PIECE FROM CAP CONTACT

6 VOLT OR 7.5 VOLT CAMERA BATTERY

.5 VOLT   MN175 OR TR175

CAP CONTACT

Step 4

Now, using your Dremel cutting blade again, cut off half of each vertical arm of the U-shaped brace that supported the brush head, which you've already removed. There should be enough of the vertical length available to you to attach the acrylic rods. Also, you may have to trim to make sure both sides are the same length.

Step 5

Cut the piece of acrylic rod into two equal lengths about 1 3/4" each. Next round off the ends of the acrylic rods with the sanding attachment on your Dremel or with sandpaper.

Step 6

Using your Dremel large-diameter drill bit, grind out a *slight* indentation at the bottoms of both acrylic rods, opposite the rounded tips. The indents you're making should fit over the LEDs and allow the rods to sit snugly over them. Now, use a light-grade sandpaper to frost the entire length of the acrylic rod so that it's no longer clear, but simply translucent. In this way it will diffuse the light from the blue LEDs.

Step 7

Pull the wires from the switch inside the handle through the top of the handle and through the tops of the arms of the U-brace to where you will seat the LEDs.

Step 8

Now it's time to wire the LEDs to the switch and battery and solder the connections. First attach the wires from the switch and battery assembly to the LEDs, making sure you attach positive to positive and negative to negative. Wire the LEDs in series through the curved bottom part of the U-brace. Set each LED just inside the tips of each arm of the U-brace. If you have to hollow out the tip of each arm just a bit to get a good seat, use your Dremel large-diameter drill bit to build yourself a curved indentation. When the circuit is complete, solder the entire circuit so that the connections are secure. Finally, glue the LEDs to the front of the handle so that the lights are just barely exposed.

Step 9

Once the LEDs have been glued in place and the circuit is completely soldered, spray paint the outsides of the two halves of the brush and set aside to dry.

Step 10

Once the paint is dry, fit the two halves of the brush handle together and, if necessary, sand down any rough spots caused by paint buildup along the seams. Now snap the two halves together and replace the rubber O-rings by working them into place gently with your screwdriver. Now you can fit the acrylic tubing to the edges of the U-brace arms so that they cover the LEDs. Make sure they fit and sand around the edges where necessary to make sure there are no gaps in the seam. If they fit securely, glue the acrylic rods in place over the LED and let dry. When the acrylic rods are dry, glue the Starfleet Medical Insignia to the handle.

Step 11

Replace the batteries in the handle and turn on the switch. You'll see how the beams from the blue LEDs are diffused by the frosted acrylic and disperse an eerie glow against your skin.

Acknowledgments

MICHAEL WESTMORE

I have often said *Star Trek* has afforded me the greatest creative and artistic challenges in the universe. Every day is a new beginning for me and the incredible makeup and hairstyling crew. With pride I say I love my job, and I love my family for all their encouragement and support. I want to acknowledge and thank my wife, Marion, my son, Michael, Jr., and my daughters, Michele and McKenzie, without whose support and love I certainly could not do the job I do, nor could I have written this book.

ALAN SIMS

A property master can only do his job when he has great producers and the support of the entire cast, staff, and crew. Therefore, I have to count myself as among the lucky because nowhere in Hollywood is there a better team than at *Star Trek*. Accordingly, I want to acknowledge and thank Rick Berman, Brannon Braga, Jeri Taylor, Michael Piller, Bob Justman, Merri Howard, David Livingston, Ken Biller, Joe Menosky, Peter Lauritson, Bryan Fuller, Dan Curry, Ron B. Moore, Mitch Suskin, Art Codron, Dawn Velazquez, Rick Kolbe, Brad Yacobian, Jerry Fleck, Suzi Shimizu, Herman Zimmerman, Penny Juday, Richard James, Louise Dorton, Rick Sternbach, Michael Okuda, Denise Okuda, Andy Probert, James Van Over, Dave Rossi, Maril Davis, Michael O'Halloran, Nicole Gravett, Eric Norman, Jim Mees, Fernando Sepulveda, Bob DelaGarza, Lisa Rich, Josée Normand, Mike Westmore, Bob Blackman, Carol Kunz, Tim Shull, Tom Siegel, Dennis Madalone. To my talented and diligent Prop Crew, Charles Russo and John Nesterowicz, a special added thanks is in order, and to the entire cast of *Star Trek: Voyager*, thank you. My job demands that I never stop thinking about props, even when I'm off the set. For my family, whose love and understanding support my craziness when I stop in the supermarket and stare at a strange looking purple vegetable for more than ten minutes and say, "I've got it," I say special thanks. To my sons James and Sean Sims and to my love Donna and her children Andrew, Amanda, and Bryan, thank you.

BRADLEY M. LOOK AND WILLIAM J. BIRNES

We want to thank our families for putting up with us while we fussed and fretted over researching and writing this book. It was fun, but it wasn't easy. We couldn't have done it without their support. Brad wants to thank his special friends Clayton Stang and Cynthia Brandt and Bill wants to thank his wife, Nancy.

All of the authors acknowledge the help and life-support of our editor, Margaret Clark at Pocket Books, who is the single reason this book exists.